A BIG CUMULONIMBUS CLOUD LOOMED AHEAD. IT looked like a black anvil floating in the sky. There was no time to go around.

Ethan led the way. He plowed straight inside. His cameras went gray. His radar started bouncing mirror images all over his screens.

Must have been the static charge inside the cloud.

He and his wingmates emerged in a clear space—

And ran smack into the middle of the enemy squadron of bees.

Flashes and blurred colors made a jumble of his displays, disorienting Ethan for a split second as he fumbled at the controls.

A bee clipped him and sent the wasp spinning.

Those bees hadn't gone after Angel and Madison. Somehow they'd fooled Ethan's sensors.

This ambush was for them!

Also by Eric Nylund

The Resisters

The Resisters 2: Sterling Squadron

The Resisters 3: Titan Base

THE RESISTERS 4

OPERATION INFERNO

. . .

ERIC NYLUND

A YEARLING BOOK

Text copyright © 2013 by Eric Nylund
Cover art copyright © 2013 by Jason Chan

All rights reserved. Published in the United States by Yearling, an imprint of Random House Children's Books, a division of Random House, Inc., New York.

Yearling and the jumping horse design are registered trademarks of Random House, Inc.

Visit us on the Web! randomhouse.com/kids

Educators and librarians, for a variety of teaching tools, visit us at
RHTeachersLibrarians.com

Library of Congress Cataloging-in-Publication Data
Nylund, Eric S.
Operation Inferno / Eric Nylund. — First Yearling edition.
p. cm. — (The resisters ; 4)
Summary: "Ethan and his team must infiltrate a heavily guarded Ch'zar industrial complex to stop the aliens from attacking the Resisters' new base." — Provided by publisher.
ISBN 978-0-307-97855-4 (pbk.) — ISBN 978-0-375-97128-0 (lib. bdg.) —
ISBN 978-0-375-98119-7 (ebook)
[1. Science fiction. 2. Extraterrestrial beings—Fiction. 3. Leadership—Fiction.
4. Brainwashing—Fiction.] I. Title.
PZ7.N9948Ope 2013 [Fic]—dc23 2013004689

Printed in the United States of America

10 9 8 7 6 5 4 3 2 1

First Yearling Edition 2013

° ° ° CONTENTS ° ° °

° ° ° SITUATION UPDATE ° ° °
Filed by Lieutenant Blackwood, Ethan G.,
commanding officer of Sterling Squadron,
eight days after the destruction of the Seed
Bank base.

SUMMARY: Seed Bank survivors continue to explore base of unknown origins.

GOALS *(in order of priority):* Find food, fuel, ammunition, and other resources to survive.

Continue to resist the alien Ch'zar.

Investigate base communication system to infiltrate Ch'zar satellite network.

Discover who built this complex (we've named it Titan Base), and why it was built and then abandoned.

DETAILS: See previous entries on how this all started—how fifty years ago, the Ch'zar took over the world and kids like myself formed a Resistance to fight them.

The Ch'zar then discovered our previous base, the Seed Bank, and bombed it into rubble, killing the adults or recruiting them to their cause.

I'm not sure what happened to the other kid pilots, but considering the overwhelming odds that we faced, I have to assume that they are dead or have been captured as well.

So, that leaves us, on our own, to fight this war.

I.C.E. and Pilot situation
From the seed bank:

Sergeant Felix Winter—piloting the Gladiator-class rhinoceros beetle I.C.E. Big Blue has minor structural damage throughout exoskeleton. Supplements and the insect's natural healing should repair this over time.

Corporal Madison Irving—her reconnaissance dragonfly I.C.E. is in good working order but low on the special high-energy diet required for its upkeep.

Private Paul Hicks—in the Crusher green praying mantis. Some hydraulic irregularities, which he's checking. No significant damage.

Recruits from the prison
sterling Reform school:

Emma Blackwood (my sister)—piloting the assault-scout hybrid ladybug I.C.E. The unit is low on missiles. Searching for suitable replacements.

Oliver Pondsmith—minor hull cracks to his silver cockroach I.C.E. Minor energy cell coolant leak (think it's fixed, but watching it closely).

Kristov Worton—his red locust is in good shape.

Lee Princeton—housefly I.C.E. needs major work on camera systems. Most of its lenses were shattered. Luckily there are lots of replacement parts in the base's flight bay.

Angel (no last name on file, and she's not telling)—Nightmare-class black wasp I.C.E. In good shape, although it's acting a bit aggressive. Note: check programming.

The refugees from Santa Blanca:

These are mostly people from my school's Grizzlies soccer team. They have no I.C.E.s assigned. They are: Bobby Buckman, Sara Smyth, Leo Jacard, Rick D'Oro, Marta Paseo, and Kyle Evans.

These Santa Blanca refugees are just trying to catch up. They're more numb than anything else.

The original Seed Bank pilots have more training and combat experience than the others (even me), but they're traumatized. They saw the destruction of their homes and the deaths of their parents and loved ones. They have to deal with that.

The Sterling recruits are in the best mental shape. They're following orders for now, but I get the feeling they're unsure about everything.

They've all followed me into battle. We've faced impossible odds together. Even death. They believe in me.

But do *I*?

A MILLION TONS OF RUST

ETHAN BLACKWOOD SET THE REPORT HE'D BEEN writing on his desk. Well, technically, it wasn't *his* desk. He ran a hand over the worn plastic simulated wood-grain surface. He was just borrowing the thing.

Like the room. Like the entire base.

He sat alone in a huge office. The walls were covered with dead computer screens, bookshelves (minus the books), and blank spots that might've once been covered with pictures or maps. The room was three times the size of Colonel Winter's office.

He glanced at the status report he'd just written.

Sterling Squadron was falling apart. Sure, this base had saved their lives. They'd all gotten a second chance. But to do what? Fight the entire Ch'zar alien race by themselves?

Impossible odds were one thing. Ethan's stomach churned. He'd faced impossible odds before—and won.

This time, though, there was *zero* chance of winning.

Not without the Seed Bank and all its resources and technology. And not without Colonel Winter or Dr. Irving.

Ethan buried his face in his hands. He'd been strong for the last few days. Now, he was exhausted.

Over the last few months, he'd come to think of the secret Resister base, the Seed Bank, as home.

Dr. Irving, and in some ways even Colonel Winter, had been like parents. He didn't think they loved him or Emma like their real parents, but they *had* cared. He knew they would've rather died than betray him. But if the adult Resisters from the Seed Bank had been captured, then their minds would now be part of the alien collective. The Ch'zar would know his tactics, tricks, everything.

He took a deep breath and squeezed his eyes shut to keep back the tears.

The colonel and the doctor always knew what they were doing when it came to fighting the aliens. No one was here now to help Ethan make the hardest decisions of his life.

Ethan pulled a photo from the stacks of technical manuals piled on the desk. It was the picture he and Emma had found at Titan Base. It was as if the picture had been waiting for them there for fifteen years.

The yellowed photograph was of Melinda and Franklin Blackwood, their parents. They wore white uniforms with silver infinity symbols on the lapels. The picture had been taken here. Ethan could see the computer displays and panels in the background.

But then they'd left. They had to have known about the Ch'zar, and yet they'd picked Santa Blanca to raise him and his sister. How could they have done that, knowing their children's minds would be at risk when they became teenagers?

Being a teenager and hitting puberty was when the big changes in brain chemistry happened and the Ch'zar's mind-control powers got you.

Ethan traced the edges of his parents' faces in the photograph. There was so much more to his parents than he knew.

They'd abandoned him and Emma when the Ch'zar got suspicious about them, but Melinda and Franklin Blackwood had left their children a trail of clues to find this old base, too.

Ethan had come full circle.

If only he could talk to his parents. He had a million questions.

A knock on the door snapped him back to reality.

Ethan hastily slid the picture under his paperwork. "Come in," he said.

The door opened, and Felix entered the office. He snapped off a quick salute. He carried a rolled-up blueprint.

Ethan's best friend had bloodshot eyes. His massive shoulders sagged. It looked like he'd aged a year in the last week.

"Status?" Ethan asked.

Felix stared past Ethan.

Ethan bet Felix was thinking of his mother's office back at the Seed Bank. How could his friend *not* think about his mother?

Ethan stood and walked around his desk. He wouldn't let his friend down by being weak.

"Status, Sergeant?" he asked again.

Felix's eyes refocused. "Right."

Felix marched to a table covered with maps of the American Southwest and unrolled the blueprint. It showed corridors and rooms, huge fusion reactors, coolant pumps the size of houses—all hooked to a jagged line that said NOT TO SCALE, which then connected to a line of satellite dishes.

They'd found the plans for the base's communication system the day before. Ethan had ordered that section explored. It had looked promising. They needed electronic eyes and ears out there to see what the Ch'zar were plotting.

The great thing about Titan Base was that it was *big*. There were a half dozen fighter jet bays with parts, ammunition, and fuel for their I.C.E.s. There were food warehouses full of freeze-dried meals that could feed an army for a hundred years (although after having tasted one, Ethan thought starving might have been better). There was a hospital. There were enough beds and bathrooms for a thousand people.

Had this place been built for the Fourth World War, before the Ch'zar invaded fifty years ago? It seemed *at least* that old, with rusting pipes and tunnels. Some sections were filled with mold and sealed off.

Sterling Squadron had only explored a fraction of the place in the last eight days.

Ethan had no clue how big it actually was. Who knew what else was there?

"I sent Lee and Oliver here." Felix pointed to a room labeled SATELLITE RELAY CONTROL. "They turned on the system with a jerry-rigged power supply. But there's no signal."

"A signal from the satellite dishes?" Ethan tapped the schematics of a dozen satellite dishes. "They can't still be out there, intact, after all these years, can they?"

Felix stood straighter. "That's why we sent a sortie to look."

Ethan waved his hand and nodded. "Yeah, I remember. Sorry."

They'd discussed this the night before. If they could connect to those dishes, they might be able to tap into the satellite network in orbit. Ethan was so tired he was forgetting critical things . . . like dangerous missions into unknown airspace to find critical communication installations.

"Who'd you send?"

"Madison. And Angel."

Ethan flashed him a hard look. Those two didn't get along.

"Their wasp and dragonfly are the best ones for the mission," Felix explained. "Those I.C.E.s have stealth."

"It's not the I.C.E.s I'm worried about. You sure those two won't blast each other out of the air?"

"I've talked with Madison," Felix told him. "She's okay."

Ethan crossed his arms over his chest. This scouting mission should have never slipped his mind. His pilots' lives were at stake. All their lives were at stake every time they went out.

After the Ch'zar had reduced the Seed Bank mountain into gravel, Ethan had no doubt that if they ever found this place, they'd bomb old Titan Base until a million tons of rust buried the Resisters alive.

Secrecy was their first, best, and maybe their *only* dependable weapon.

Felix made a motion to set his big hand on Ethan's shoulder, but then halted. "You okay, sir?"

"I'm fine. Just tired. Nothing . . . weird, if that's what you're asking."

Weird as in Ethan and Emma had heard the mental

song of the Ch'zar on their last mission. Emma had even dominated and controlled an unpiloted enemy I.C.E. and saved their lives. It wasn't normal, though, and it had everyone in Sterling on pins and needles.

Felix looked Ethan over and gave him a quick nod. They'd saved each other a dozen times before. He trusted Ethan or, at least, trusted himself to know if Ethan had fallen under the influence of the Ch'zar.

The big guy swayed. He leaned against the table to steady himself.

Felix was pushing it. Ethan couldn't remember the last time his friend had slept. He bet Felix was trying to avoid the nightmares.

When Ethan dreamed, he saw the Seed Bank blowing up, heard screams over the radio, and felt bugs crawling on his skin.

"Are *you* okay?" Ethan asked.

Felix blinked and set his large hand on the table. "Just need breakfast. More fifty-year-old rehydrated eggs. Yummy." He glanced at his wristwatch. "Madison's due to report in five minutes. We should get up to the Command Center."

Paul Hicks burst into Ethan's office. He was out of breath. Sweat plastered his sandy-red hair over his eyes and he brushed it away, revealing the three long scars that ran down the left side of his face.

Paul didn't salute Ethan. He didn't even look at him, as if Felix was the only person in the room.

There had been friction between Paul and Ethan since they'd met at the Seed Bank. Paul couldn't let go that Ethan was just as good a pilot. And he definitely couldn't deal with Ethan being a better leader.

Felix pursed his lips and nodded toward Ethan as if to tell Paul to give their commanding officer a little respect.

Paul shook his head, then caught his breath. "Madison . . . ," he panted, "found something."

Ethan took a step closer to Paul, all thoughts of how much he hated him forgotten.

"Or actually . . . ," Paul continued, "some*thing* found her and Angel."

∘ ∘ ∘ 2 ∘ ∘ ∘

CENTER OF COMMAND

ETHAN RAN UP SEVEN FLIGHTS OF STAIRS. There was an elevator, but after a few decades of its being out of service, he didn't trust it.

He sprinted through the vault doors to Titan Base's Command Center.

A breeze cooled him off. The room was so big it had its own wind currents.

When he and Emma had first found the base and rebooted the fusion reactors, they'd used what they *thought* was the Command Center. It turned out that it had been the emergency auxiliary control room.

It was only after three days of exploring that they'd found *this* place, the real Command Center.

Like everything else in Titan Base it was, well . . . titanic.

The room was its own subterranean world. It was hard to say exactly how big it was. Ethan counted paces the first time he'd crossed it. One hundred sixty. Almost a city block. Four Northside Elementary gymnasiums could've fit in the place.

What made the space really hard to fathom was its height.

Ethan couldn't see the ceiling. He had even used binoculars.

There were beams the size of redwoods up there with a thousand lights that could glow soft like a moon or dazzle with the brilliance of full daylight. Currently the lights were set to MOON GLOW.

When they'd found this place, it'd been full of cobwebs and a layer of dust a quarter inch thick. That stuff vanished over the next few days as they used the room and brought more power online.

Ethan got the creepy feeling that something was living up there in the shadows . . . cleaning the place when they weren't looking.

The most impressive thing about the Command Center, though, was its displays.

Acres of curved walls projected maps and computer screens.

Ethan had walked up close and never cast a shadow on those walls. He couldn't see a single pixel either— even when he got so close he smudged the glass surface with his nose.

His sister was there, hunched over computer controls, keyboards, trackballs, and gel pads. Emma's hands flew over them. In response, maps zoomed across the walls and patchworked into a map of the entire world.

And in *this* room, the entire world seemed to fit just right.

Ethan jogged to her. She didn't look up from the controls. She'd wrapped her long braid around her neck so it wasn't in the way of her hands. She held up a finger to stop him while she tapped in the last command.

"Paul said Madison found something? Or something found her? Are she and Angel safe?"

"There," she said, and turned to him. "All online. And yes, they're fine. For the moment. I think."

Ethan hardly recognized his sister. He hadn't seen his old joking, shoulder-punching sibling since she got here. She was all business. This was how he'd seen her when she had procrastinated studying for a final exam, then crammed in the last ten minutes, learning everything at once.

"When Madison and Angel reconnected the first communication array," Emma told him, "the rest of the system woke up. Lines are repairing themselves. The old network is at eighty-five percent capacity and increasing. We've got nearly *global* coverage."

"Global coverage of what?"

Emma narrowed her dark eyes. "Everything, dummy."

She glanced at Felix and Paul as they entered the cavernous room. They marveled at the huge images of the twirling world, then approached.

"I mean everything . . . sir," Emma said in a deliberately respectful tone.

"The Titan Base system has hijacked the Ch'zar satellite network, too," she said. "As far as I can tell—*without* the aliens knowing. So, now we can see everything they do." She blinked a few times, turned in a circle, and took in the magnificent hundred-thousand-foot view of Earth around her. "Pretty cool, huh?"

Ethan frowned. It *was* cool. But he wasn't sure a hack into the alien sensor system wasn't being detected by the Ch'zar. The technicians at the Seed Bank could only ever manage a few key satellites at a time.

"I'm monitoring system feedback here." Emma tapped a control panel. "Not a single pulse. They don't know we're inside."

He hated when she did that: practically read his mind.

Ethan noticed a glass-covered switch at her station. It was outlined in red-striped tape and said BREAK IN CASE OF EMERGENCY.

"That severs the network connection," Emma told him. "Just in case the Ch'zar find out we're in their system. It's like the people who built this place were just as scared about them as we are."

Ethan nodded.

But that didn't quite make sense. This place was so old it had to have been built *before* the Ch'zar came to Earth.

Felix and Paul leaned on Emma's computer station.

"Nice," Felix said, admiring the communication controls. He stepped closer to Emma.

She smiled at him, and then her face smoothed back to business mode.

Paul edged between Emma and Ethan. He tapped

in a few commands. "I'll bring up Madison's feed," he said to Felix. "You're going to want to see this."

Emma glared at Paul's intrusion into her space.

He ignored her.

Ethan held back the urge to punch Paul in the face . . . only because he wanted to see what was going on with Madison and Angel out there.

"Got them." Paul's voice was thick with concentration.

Static fuzzed over the walls.

"Oops," Paul said.

Emma sighed. "Boys . . . ," she muttered.

She shoved Paul out of the way and took over. She adjusted the images and magnified North America. With one hand, she spun a control and zoomed into the Southwestern region. A layer of satellites in low-Earth orbit flashed by and the viewpoint descended. Desert dunes and chalky mountains crystallized into focus.

When Ethan had seen the Seed Bank technicians hijack the Ch'zar's satellites, he'd viewed bits and pieces of the world from up high. There were usually blackout zones. But Ethan may have severely underestimated the aliens' strategic overview. They could see everything from up there.

The view continued to swoop downward until wisps of clouds resolved.

"This is six thousand feet," Emma said.

Ethan felt like a weather balloon, hovering higher than his I.C.E. could've flown over a wide expanse of desert. He saw a hazy Gulf of California on the western horizon.

"There." Felix pointed at three o'clock. A slight smear appeared in blue skies.

"That's not Madison," Ethan said. "She wouldn't break stealth protocols."

"Unless she's in trouble," Felix said.

Or it was Angel. But Ethan kept silent about that possibility.

"It's not them," Paul said. He fiddled with a dial. The part of the wall they were looking at expanded a hundred times.

The smear grew into a life-sized I.C.E.—fifteen feet from mandibles to stinger.

It was a giant bee, but not like any bee Ethan had seen before.

The combat bumblebee units used by the Resisters were matte black and golden yellow. Their undersides were painted sky blue and white for camouflage. They usually gripped a half-ton bomb in their legs.

The Ch'zar bee units were plain gray titanium with heavy armor plates and usually had missile racks on their hind legs in place of pollen sacks.

But this thing was just plain . . . weird.

It had no obvious weapons: no plasma beam-emitter antennae, no missiles, no smoldering stinger lasers. And the colors? It looked as if the giant insect had tangled with a paint store and lost. Its exoskeleton was a collection of smudges—sky blue, gray, olive green, and black

Ethan blinked. It almost hurt to look at the thing because the edges got lost.

He squinted. He thought it was one of the larger bumblebee species. But the usual armor plates and combat barbs had been stripped off.

So, how was this thing supposed to fight?

If it was a stealth unit, the Ch'zar sure picked a bulky species to do the job.

"We spotted this about ten minutes ago," Emma said. "It's no big deal. The Ch'zar have units scattered all over the place."

"That's no Ch'zar unit I've ever seen," Paul told her.

"And check this out." He tapped a few buttons. "I recorded its flight path."

"You didn't tell me that," Emma said.

Paul shrugged. "I don't have to tell you everything I do. Besides, you've barely got your wings—what do you know anyway?"

Emma's mouth dropped open.

Felix took a step toward Paul, one hand curling into a fist.

Ethan touched Felix's arm and shook his head. Now wasn't the time. Paul would get what was coming to him—but after Ethan's pilots were safely back at base.

Two curved lines winked onto the map.

The first traced Madison's and Angel's flight path as they approached the hidden satellite dishes and then arced back to Titan Base. That was perfectly normal.

But the other line showed the trajectory of the strange bee. At first, it meandered in what Ethan suspected was a zigzag search pattern. Then it paused, turned, and started *toward* the Resister I.C.E.s.

"It's following them," Paul declared.

"That's not possible," Ethan whispered. "Madison and Angel are stealthed."

"It has to be a coincidence," Emma said, suddenly

sounding not so sure. "Besides, our girls are a hundred miles away from that thing. It'll never catch—"

A dot appeared on-screen two hundred miles ahead of Madison's and Angel's I.C.E.s.

The viewscreen automatically zoomed on those dots, and warning icons popped alongside the magnified section.

Six more strangely painted bees came into focus.

The computer automatically plotted the bees' projected course . . . which intercepted the Resister scouts.

Ethan blinked, then sprinted for the Command Center exit.

He didn't have to tell Emma, Paul, or Felix. They were already ahead of him, dashing for the I.C.E. launch bay.

They all recognized an ambush when they saw one.

○ ○ ○ 3 ○ ○ ○

AMBUSH

THE I.C.E. FLIGHT DECK WAS A CANYON WITH walls that stretched to massive sliding doors twenty stories overhead. The topside of those doors was the camouflaged surface of a dry lakebed.

Sometimes Ethan couldn't help but think of Titan Base as a ginormous set of natural wonders, like Carlsbad Caverns, rather than something man-made.

Hydraulic lines ten feet in diameter powered the lake doors. Support struts held the entire thing aloft, making it look like part of Arches National Park, which Ethan had seen pictures of in school.

Red lights on the flight deck whirled and flashed. Emma must have set the scramble signal before they'd sprinted up here.

The Resisters' nine I.C.E.s were lined up on the landing deck. They looked like toys compared to everything else . . . and the people swarming over them, like ants.

Bobby Buckman and the other Santa Blanca kids were there. Felix had them on repair and maintenance training, which is where every normal Resister pilot started (*not* like the crash course Ethan had gotten).

Kristov was there, too, supervising. He was an inch shorter than Felix but had twenty pounds of muscle on him. Big guy. Ethan was glad Kristov was on their side.

Kristov approached Ethan, Felix, Paul, and Emma. He straightened his large frame and saluted. "I.C.E.s ready for launch, Lieutenant," he told Ethan.

Bobby, Leo, Sara, and the other Santa Blanca refugees trotted up, too. Bobby wiped greasy hands on his coveralls, swept his dark curly hair from his face, and stepped forward. "Is this anything we can help with, Ethan—I mean, sir?" Bobby said.

Bobby and the others had clocked a few hours'

simulation in I.C.E. cockpits with the bugs in *dream* mode. They were all itching to get out there and prove themselves.

Ethan knew how they felt. They wanted some payback for losing their parents. But he had way more potential pilots now than they had I.C.E.s. He could only afford to send out experienced pilots, especially on a combat sortie.

"Not this time," Ethan told him. "Madison and Angel might be in trouble."

Bobby nodded. "I get it. Good luck, and burn a few Ch'zar for us." He and the others stepped out of the way. They all saluted.

Ethan flushed. He could get used to giving orders and not having them questioned. The people he'd saved from Santa Blanca and Sterling (apart from Angel, who was crazy) simply acknowledged him as their leader.

He'd earned that recognition, and he'd have to *keep on* earning it, but it sure was nice.

Ethan snapped off a salute to the flight crew and ran to his wasp.

The truck-sized biomechanical insect shuffled to face him. Its antennae waggled, sensing its pilot. The abdomen cockpit hatch hissed open, inviting Ethan inside.

Sometimes it was easy to forget that the I.C.E.s weren't just mechanical. They were part organic and alive, with primitive yet overwhelmingly strong feelings.

His wasp had recognized him.

Ethan checked the bug's recent repairs. They had chitin rebonding supplies from the secret Resister cache they'd raided before finding Titan Base.

The major cracks in his wasp's gold-and-black-striped exoskeleton were gone. Ethan ran a finger over the faint seam in the armor.

On contact he sunk into the wasp's mind. It was happy to see him. No . . . it was anticipating flying and fighting. It was hungry for violence.

Was that a bug thing? Or something all Ch'zar minds shared?

He withdrew his hand and went back to the inspection.

The repair job wasn't perfect. The coloration didn't quite match, and there were spots where the sensor hairs had been burned off. But the wasp wasn't going to rattle apart if they hit Mach speeds.

Good enough.

Ethan clambered into the cockpit.

The hatch shut as soon as he cleared the threshold.

Clusters of computer screens and displays flickered to life. Ethan had a full 360-degree view. Interior breathing vents opened and puffed cold air. Gloppy acceleration gel flooded the nooks and crannies as he slipped his legs and arms into control armatures.

Indicator lights were all green, except one stubborn afterburner regulator that flickered amber, then green again.

"I'm ready," Ethan said on the short-range radio channel. "Status, everyone?"

"Good here," Felix reported from his hulking blue rhinoceros beetle.

"Same," Emma said, as her ladybug's shell split apart and its wings ruffled out.

Paul flicked his green status light on Ethan's panel, apparently not able to talk to Ethan even over the radio.

"Got a low-pressure reading on the starboard wing gimbal," Kristov said with a grunt. "It's okay. I can fly."

"We can't afford to fall back in the middle of a fight if your locust's wing seizes," Ethan told him. "You're grounded, pending repairs, Kristov. I'm sorry."

A huge sigh blasted over the radio. "Yes, sir."

"Open the doors," Ethan ordered.

The deck crew scrambled to the hydraulic controls. A rumble shook the entire bay. Overhead sunlight spilled into the flight deck as the lakebed doors parted.

Ethan's wasp, Paul's praying mantis, Emma's ladybug, and Felix's beetle took off—soaring up and out into a bright gold desert sky.

Ethan plotted a course on his flight computer. He traced the shortest path to those unknown units zeroing in on Angel and Madison.

He considered breaking radio silence, sending a coded signal to Angel and Madison, but decided against it. That could reveal his position to the Ch'zar. Maybe get them all captured.

They could reach those enemy fliers before they got to his scouts—but they'd have to *move*.

"Lock jet and prime afterburners," Ethan commanded.

Exoskeleton segments withdrew on his port and starboard sides. Jet engines spun up and *thunk*ed in place.

Acceleration squished Ethan into his seat.

The flight computer projected it would take only a few minutes to intercept the targets.

He double-checked the wasp's laser stinger. It held a 90 percent charge. Not perfect, but good enough.

He cycled through the hydraulic system on his status board. He didn't want any surprises if he went hand-to-hand combat. All green.

Ethan's hand hovered of its own accord over a small hexagonal panel. It was covered with Ch'zar icons that glowed brighter the closer he came to them.

He and Emma had somehow gotten the ability to decipher Ch'zar icons. The weird alien dot-and-dash hieroglyphics and geometric shapes just suddenly clicked in their minds.

His finger itched to press one icon. It translated loosely as *Exoskeleton Destiny Overdrive*.

Dr. Irving had once told Ethan that the Ch'zar had the technology to make the molecules in I.C.E. armor superdense. It might make the wasp invincible in a fight. He bet it'd cost lots of energy, though.

Odd that the Resister techs or trainers had never mentioned the feature. Maybe it didn't work. Or maybe they didn't understand it completely.

Ethan decided not to mess with it now.

He checked the squadron's status once more. Green across the board.

He smiled.

Four veteran Resister pilots who'd kicked the Ch'zar Collective's butts versus just a few units—what looked like *unarmed* Ch'zar units, no less.

This wasn't even going to be a contest.

Still, if they were so helpless, why was the enemy dead set on an intercept course with Angel and Madison?

Something didn't add up.

He glanced at his navigation screen. Seven minutes to contact.

A big cumulonimbus cloud loomed ahead. It looked like a black anvil floating in the sky. There was no time to go around.

Ethan led the way. He plowed straight inside. His cameras went gray. His radar started bouncing mirror images all over his screens.

Must have been the static charge inside the cloud.

He and his wingmates emerged in a clear space—

And ran smack into the middle of the enemy squadron of bees.

Flashes and blurred colors made a jumble of his

displays, disorienting Ethan for a split second as he fumbled at the controls.

A bee clipped him and sent the wasp spinning.

Those bees hadn't gone after Angel and Madison. Somehow they'd fooled Ethan's sensors.

This ambush was for them!

∘∘∘ 4 ∘∘∘

BIGGEST THREAT

ETHAN WRESTLED WITH THE CONTROLS TO HALT the gut-jarring tumble. He did it. Then he blinked, trying to stop his head from spinning, too . . . and trying to find a target to blast.

His computer displays were full of bees—appearing and vanishing in iron-gray cloud cover. The enemy seemed to be everywhere at once, way more than the original seven he'd seen on the satellite image back at base.

How was that possible?

It didn't matter. He had to start fighting before it was over for him.

He moved toward the closest bee, laser-firing rings locking on his combat screen.

A proximity warning blared.

Ethan instinctively pulled back on the controls.

A three-ton bee flashed right where he would have been a microsecond later.

The cloud moved. Dense mist surrounded him. His visuals were down to a hundred feet.

His heart pounded so hard he thought it'd jump out of his chest.

Why would seven unarmed bees take on four combat I.C.E.s? It was suicide.

Not that the Ch'zar cared about individual deaths. Maybe they were there to slow the Resisters down while reinforcements showed up.

Or there could be more. Lots more.

Ethan decided to blow them all to smithereens. Get within short-range radio distance of Angel and Madison—and get them all out of there, fast. They could figure it all out later.

"Engage at will!" Ethan shouted over the squad channel. "Just be careful because—"

His wasp got slammed from the underside. Ethan's teeth clacked shut.

The wasp had grabbed at something, but it bounced off and was already out of reach.

Another bee rocketed at him out of the swirling clouds, afterburners blazing.

Ethan cut his own afterburners.

The bee missed and vanished into the mist.

If Ethan hadn't stopped, that thing would have collided with him. And at those speeds it would've ripped his wings off.

These guys were crazy. And good.

Meanwhile, Felix blasted every bee within range. His plasma vaporized clouds around him in a quarter-mile swath—but he still kept missing!

Ethan couldn't believe it. Sure, Felix had missed before. But never multiple targets clustered at this short of a range.

The bees moved like they could defy the laws of physics. They jinked back and forth and barrel-rolled to one side a split second before the class-C particle emitter antennae of the rhinoceros beetle ignited the air.

Paul's Crusher praying mantis chased after the color-speckled bees, desperately trying to snatch one out of the air. He was running one down, getting closer and closer . . . but also getting farther from the rest of the squadron.

"Paul, break, and get back here," Ethan ordered. "They're setting you up."

The praying mantis hovered.

Paul probably chewed back some insult, but he must have realized that Ethan was right—that he was headed into a trap—because he circled back.

Ethan upped his estimation of the bees.

With a chill, he realized that luring the Resisters' I.C.E.s away from one another in this cloud cover was what *he* would have done.

Emma's ladybug let loose a salvo of rocket-propelled grenades. They *whoosh*ed at a bee harassing her I.C.E.

The bee hit its afterburners trying to outpace the explosives. *Good luck*, Ethan thought.

Flashes erupted from the bee's hind legs, where pollen sacks would have normally been.

They were decoy flares. Dr. Irving had explained them once to Ethan. He'd said he'd been experimenting with *old* technologies for Resister I.C.E.s. The heat from the burning magnesium confused targeting sensors.

Every rocket-propelled grenade exploded harmlessly in the air.

The bee got away clean.

Ethan didn't want to think what this meant, but he couldn't help it. Did the Ch'zar have Dr. Irving?

No. He refused to believe it.

Dr. Irving died at the Seed Bank.

But how else to explain the Ch'zar's new tactics?

"Group on me," Ethan ordered. "Full defensive posture."

Paul's mantis, Felix's rhinoceros beetle, and Emma's ladybug moved to Ethan and hovered in a tight wedge, each facing a different direction.

The bees were still out of visual range, hiding in the churning clouds, where Ethan's radar was bouncing back a few dozen images all over the place. Without visuals, he had to depend on his instruments . . . which couldn't be trusted.

"What are we doing here?" Paul growled. "We're sitting ducks."

"Madison and Angel," Ethan told him. "We need to keep these bees distracted and off them until they're safe."

"I'm more worried about *us* being safe," Paul muttered.

"What the heck *are* those things?" Felix asked. The beetle's huge wings were a blur of thunder and turbulence. "One bounced off your wasp, Ethan. Not a scratch on its shell."

"Not *what*," Emma said. "*Who*. They're not fighting like Ch'zar. They're erratic, fighting like, well, humans."

"If they are humans, uncontrolled humans," Paul said, "then why are they trying to kill us?"

"Cut the chatter," Ethan said. "I have to figure this out."

He scanned the billowing vapors surrounding them. Inside the cloud, tendrils of mist swirled. Ethan found it hypnotic.

There could have been any number of bees waiting for them to break their defensive formation.

"If we run," Ethan murmured to himself, "then they'll pick us off. We won't even see them coming."

"So remove the clouds," Emma said.

From her impatient tone, Ethan could almost hear the "duh" she left out of her statement.

Emma's ladybug launched two salvos of rocket-propelled grenades. The air flashed and clouds boiled away in front of her, clearing a space five hundred feet wide.

"Nice!" Felix cried. He charged his beetle's plasma emitter antennae and let loose a column of superheated ionized gas.

The cotton puff clouds disappeared so fast it looked as if they leaped out of the way to avoid getting scalded.

Ethan added his stinger's laser heat to the offensive, painting the wall of iron gray ahead of him. More cloud vapors curled and vanished.

There was a cluster of five bees at five o'clock and a thousand feet higher. A perfect attack position.

Felix saw them, too. His beetle turned and launched a bolt of plasma.

The bees disappeared farther back in the cloud cover.

"Do we go after them?" Emma asked.

"Ethan? Lieutenant?" Madison's voice squawked over the squadron channel. "What's going on? What are you guys doing out here?"

Far on the edge of his radar, Ethan saw dragonfly and wasp silhouettes on an intercept course.

"Didn't you see them?" Paul asked.

"See who?" Angel replied. "You guys are the only thing on the radar for two hundred miles."

"Form up on us," Ethan ordered. "Go radio silent."

There was a grumble from Angel . . . but then the channel was quiet.

Ethan dove lower to get out of the cloud. The squadron followed him.

All of Ethan's pilot instincts told him to stay and finish the fight. But now was not the right time to engage an unknown enemy whose technologies baffled them.

He had to get back to the base and think . . .

Because Sterling Squadron was no longer the biggest threat in the air.

∘ ∘ ∘ 5 ∘ ∘ ∘

OPEN YOUR EYES

ETHAN STOOD IN THE MIDDLE OF TITAN BASE'S stadium-like Command Center. He toweled off the last of the acceleration gel from his flight suit. The stuff kept him from getting battered and bruised (mostly) at high-g maneuvers in combat but was a real mess.

And it was hard to look dignified and in control covered in goo.

Standing at various computer stations and sitting in ultramodern curved chairs was everyone in the entire squadron, along with Bobby and the other Santa Blanca refugees.

Well, *almost* all of them were here.

Lee and Oliver were on the radio, listening in. They were still hiking back from deep within the sub-basements of Titan Base, where they'd been repairing the satellite relay.

Ethan tapped the intercom system. "You guys hear us okay?"

"Loud and clear," Lee said.

"No problem," Oliver said. He was breathing hard from the fast pace they were setting to get back.

"So let's run over it once more," Ethan said. "We're probably missing something important."

Paul shook his head as if Ethan was a complete id-iot, but this time he said nothing. Instead, he turned his back to Ethan and took in the 360-degree viewscreen.

"Angel and Madison left at sunrise," Felix told them all, starting off the recap.

"What did you see on the way out to the satellite dishes?" Ethan asked.

Madison opened her mouth to speak—but Angel jumped in first.

"There wasn't much in the air," Angel said. She shook her angular bangs from her eyes. "I mean, there was an I.C.E. or two, a mosquito spotter and a heavy lifting beetle, but no combat squadrons. I wanted to pick off that pesky mosquito, but—"

Madison interrupted her, shooting her a dirty look. "We followed stealth protocols to the letter, sir." Madison then stepped in front of Angel to address Ethan directly. She crossed her arms over her chest. "And didn't break radio silence until we saw you. There was no way we were spotted."

Angel made a mocking strangulation gesture behind Madison.

Madison whirled around and almost caught her.

Madison and Angel. He and Paul. Why were they at each other's throats?

Ethan felt the lines of tension drawing tight between them all. It was as if this ginormous room *still* wasn't big enough to contain the bad feelings.

How would Colonel Winter have handled this?

Probably by throwing them all in the brig to cool off for a few weeks. Or a few months.

Not a bad idea . . . if only Ethan didn't need every pilot he had to save the human race from the Ch'zar.

"Go on," Ethan prompted Madison.

"The Ch'zar have more ground units out than I've ever seen." Madison's forehead crinkled as she remembered. "It wasn't like it was an attack. They weren't marching anywhere. It's like the northern Appalachian Mountains where we've seen them mining. Hundreds of those industrial robots scooping up rock and ore and who knows what else and feeding it all into those huge walking smelter factories."

Ethan remembered seeing the Ch'zar mining the first day he'd learned the truth about the aliens controlling his life in Santa Blanca. Eight-legged robots had been tearing apart a mountainside. Mobile factories melted that ore on the spot. The metal was then shipped to a massive beanstalk elevator that carried the material into space.

In orbit, the Ch'zar were supposed to be building more spaceships. It was one of the reasons they'd come to planets like Earth. They needed raw materials to multiply.

Ethan imagined a swarm of army ants covering and devouring some helpless animal.

He shuddered.

Emma moved to the Command Center display controls. "We can scan the nearby regions," she said. "Look for some pattern to their actions."

"Hey, guys?" Lee's voice crackled over the intercom.

"Felix? Can you pick up your blueprints? Level twenty-three. Corridor G-422, cross section L? Uh . . . we're hearing some funny noises."

Lee was trying to sound calm, but Ethan heard the tightening in his voice. He nodded to Felix to check it out. Something was going on down there.

"One sec," Felix said. He crossed to a table and shuffled through the blueprints of the base. He found the one he was looking for and smoothed it flat.

"What kinds of noises are you hearing?" Ethan asked.

"Something moving . . . ," Lee whispered over the intercom. "Getting closer. Like hissing hydraulics. Or pistons."

Felix ran his finger over the blueprint, tracing corridors, a look of intense concentration on his face. He brightened and looked up. "Relax, Lee," he said. "There's a steam cooling system nearby. It's linked to the fusion reactors we turned on."

"Maybe . . . ," Lee said. "Wait. It stopped." He laughed. "It's so creepy down here. You can psych yourself out, I guess."

"Keep moving," Ethan told him. "We'll check it out later. The two of you just get up here ASAP."

"Roger that, sir," Lee said.

Ethan didn't like the unlit, rusty, musty corridors of Titan. There could be *anything* down there. Long-dormant I.C.E.s. Leaking radioactive coolant. Ghosts.

The whole place felt like the haunted house they'd had at his school's Halloween carnival.

"Okay," he said, breaking the spell. "Emma, you said you had a plan?"

"I sure do." She snapped her fingers and spun a control. The world map on the walls separated into pieces. "We each search a section," she explained. "We need to gather data across the entire planet. We have to think *big*, like the Collective mind of the Ch'zar, to have a chance of figuring out what they're up to."

Ethan frowned. Not because he didn't agree, though. Back at the Seed Bank this was how Dr. Irving had projected the Ch'zar explosive population growth. But the Seed Bank had had a supercomputer churning away at that data. It was going to take them hours, if not days, *if* they were lucky enough to figure out what the enemy was up to.

"It's a stupid plan," Paul said, tossing his hands up in frustration. "We should go back out, the whole squadron this time, and grab one of those bees. See what makes them tick. See who, or what, is inside, too."

Emma was icy cool. She glanced at Ethan, and he got her message. Now was not the time to blow up. He was in command and had to set an example.

But didn't he also have to set an example when people were jerks, too?

Ethan took a deep breath. "Neither idea is bad," he said to Paul and Emma. "Let's find out what we can here first, though. Maybe we'll catch a lucky break. If nothing else, we might see where those new bees are coming from."

Emma, Felix, and the others nodded at this.

Except Paul. He sneered, drawing the scars on his cheek tight.

"You're just chicken," Paul said, and jabbed a finger at Ethan.

Everyone stared at Paul and then Ethan.

Even Felix was speechless.

"I'm not chicken," Ethan said in an even tone. "But, yes, I am scared. You'd have to be a moron not to be."

Two weeks ago, Ethan would have gotten angry, taken Paul's bait, and rushed into battle to prove his courage (like he had with a stupid race through Knucklebone Canyon).

Ethan had learned, though, that courage only took him so far.

"We're in a war where we're outnumbered literally a million to one," Ethan told everyone. "We can't afford one downed I.C.E. or a single pilot or support crew out of the fight. This war can only be won by us being smarter than the enemy."

He turned to Paul and looked right through him as if he weren't there. "And that starts here. Now"—Ethan gestured to the maps—"by opening our eyes."

"I'm not staying cooped up in here," Paul said, so softly that Ethan barely heard him. "No one can stop me from flying when I—"

The intercom squawked.

Over a wash of static, Lee's voice was pitched to a panic. "Lieutenant! We see them now. There are too many. They're moving after us. They're—"

The channel went dead.

∘ ∘ ∘ 6 ∘ ∘ ∘

NIGHTMARES IN THE DARK

ETHAN CUT THROUGH THE DARKNESS WITH HIS flashlight. It had a huge reflector the size of a dinner plate and threw a cone of illumination brighter than the sun down the corridor.

The light was blocked by pipes and conduits that lined the walls, though. It made the tunnel look like it was covered with black spiderwebs. As powerful as the flashlight was, the passage was so big and so long that the bright light faded into murk after a hundred feet.

And beyond that, it was pitch-black again.

Ethan was with Emma, Bobby, and Angel in the

passage. There were several other groups converging on Lee and Oliver's last position. There were so many tunnels, air ducts, and passages down the twenty-third subbasement of Titan Base, and Lee and Oliver could be running down any of them. Or they could be still at cross section L of corridor G-422, where their last radio transmission had gone . . . dead.

Ethan gulped. He held up a hand, indicating that they hold.

He strained to hear. Something. Anything.

Next to him, Angel even stopped smacking her gum (she'd discovered crates of the stuff in the base's food vaults).

Water dripped from a pipe overhead. There was a distant hiss of steam. A clang along the wall sounded and faded back to silence.

But no voices. Not one scream for help.

Lee had said he'd heard hissing hydraulics or pistons.

There was only one other thing Ethan heard: his own heart thumping away in his chest.

He'd been through enough battles to know why. He was scared out of his mind. Aerial combat with mechanized monsters? No problem. A world invaded by aliens? He had that covered.

But being buried deep underground, surrounded by darkness—his mind was filling with the nightmares from every scary story he'd heard as a kid. He couldn't stop thinking of zombies and ghosts.

He clicked on his radio's SEND button twice. That was a status request from the other groups. Seven double clicks came back over the radio. No one said a word. It was the signal they'd agreed to ahead of time. A double click meant a-okay. Only if there were trouble or if they found Lee and Oliver would they break radio silence. If it was Ch'zar down here, he didn't want them listening in on his squadron's frequencies.

Ethan motioned Bobby closer. He pointed his finger at his own eyes, like he was going to poke them out, and then pointed at his palm.

Bobby nodded and got out his map. He folded it and turned it around, found where they were, and showed Ethan.

There were two more turns along this access tunnel, and then a straight section for a thousand feet that dumped into corridor G-422, cross section L.

What if Lee and Oliver were seriously injured? What if this were a practical joke? No way.

Ethan vowed not to think of every possibility. He

just had to keep moving. Find his people. And get them all out of this creepy place in one piece.

He motioned for his team to move ahead. They crept forward, silent.

Ethan hefted the crowbar in one hand. It was heavy, he bet deadly, if it ever cracked someone in the head. But against the growing fears in his mind . . . it felt like a toothpick. He wished he could've gotten an I.C.E. into these tunnels without wrecking the entire place.

Emma marched on his left. She carried a portable plasma welder torch that could slice though titanium like butter, nervously clicking the safety catch on the trigger.

Angel was on his right. She twirled a rivet gun on her finger like a gunslinger. The thing shot bolts of high-carbon steel with deadly accuracy. Meant to repair I.C.E.s, it was maybe *too* dangerous in *her* hands. She saw Ethan watching her and flashed him an evil grin.

Bobby had a length of heavy chain. It was simple. He looked confident with the improvised weapon.

Back at the Command Center when they'd heard Lee and Oliver in trouble, Ethan had quickly given orders—split up and converge from all directions. He'd considered going down in one mob, but they'd just get in one another's way in these tunnels if there was a fight.

Paul had started to protest, as usual, but Felix clamped his hands on Paul's shoulders, and the two had a whispered conversation. After that Paul hadn't said another word.

They'd all run to the flight deck, grabbed whatever they could to fight with, and clambered down the stairs to subbasement twenty-three.

That was an hour ago.

He had no idea if he'd find Lee and Oliver hurt . . . turned into enemies, absorbed by the Ch'zar Collective . . . or if they'd been attacked by the giant rats he'd almost convinced himself might be down there.

Another three hundred feet and they'd be at the target intersection. Ethan waved his flashlight back and forth.

Along with the pipes and silver electrical conduits on the walls was the occasional doorway. These were permanently sealed shut. They reminded Ethan of pictures he'd seen of submarine doors: an oval with a wheel in the middle.

These doors hadn't stood the test of time well. Every one they'd tried was rusted shut and not budge-able. They'd given up after the first dozen.

If they couldn't open them, Lee and Oliver wouldn't have been able to either.

The corridor's floor was an open waffle pattern of dull black metal. Sections could be pried up to get at pipes underneath. Nothing special there . . . except a few paces ahead, Ethan spotted a dent in one section.

He marched toward it, knelt, and found a dimple the size of a car tire. The steel mesh had been cratered a full hand-span deep. The edges had torn and split. The steel wasn't rusted, so this must have happened fairly recently. Something big and heavy had to have made this.

On a metal snag was a bit of black material.

Ethan set aside his flashlight and pulled it off.

It was rubber.

There was something familiar about it, especially the unmistakable odor of burned tire. He couldn't quite connect the mental dots, though.

He showed it to Emma. She furrowed her brow, sensing something, too, but then shook her head.

Ahead came a sudden scream of metal wrenching.

Ethan stood bolt upright, crowbar and flashlight in hand.

That had to be Lee or Oliver.

He forgot all thoughts of nightmares and ran forward—

Charging straight into the vaulted intersection of two corridors.

Where he stopped.

Dumbfounded.

Emma, Angel, and Bobby almost ran into him.

"What . . . ," Bobby whispered.

"How," Emma said, "did *they* find us?"

Twenty feet to Ethan's right—down corridor G-422—stood a cluster of ten robots.

They were like the ones he'd run into at the ghost city of New Taos. They balanced on a single wheel and towered ten feet tall. But these were different, because instead of parabolic antennae dishes in their hands, they had jackhammers, plasma cutting torches, or hydraulically powered claws.

And instead of a helmeted head with a single slit like the New Taos guardians, these guys each had three cameras mounted where a normal face should have been.

What held all the robots' attention was a solid steel bulkhead that had dropped and sealed off the rest of corridor G-422.

Three robots with plasma torches melted a gash in the middle of the bulkhead wall. Lines of molten steel dribbled down. At the other end of this tear, three robots grabbed the wall with claws, while the last few pounded at it with jackhammers.

Together they were slowly peeling back the steel like it was an orange rind.

One of the robots paused.

Its head swiveled toward Ethan . . . and its jackhammering subsided.

For a heartbeat, nothing happened.

Then all the other nine robots simultaneously stopped their work and turned.

Icy horror flooded through Ethan.

"Run . . . ," he whispered to his team. "Run for your lives!"

∘ ∘ ∘ 7 ∘ ∘ ∘

THEY'RE ALIVE

ETHAN BOLTED.

Bobby, Emma, and Angel were right behind him.

Just one of those robots was strong enough to paste him and the others. Ten robots? He didn't want to think about it. They'd be dead meat if they got caught.

But Ethan *had* to think about it. That's what commanders were supposed to do.

There was no way he could outrun a nuclear-powered wheeled death machine.

So Ethan skidded to a halt, turned, and raised his crowbar.

This made about as much sense as fighting an I.C.E. midair with a glider . . . but he was going to try *something* before he got flattened.

As he turned, he saw the robots maneuvering around the intersection corner. His brain vapor locked seeing the tons of metal men push and shove to get ahead of one another in order to crush him.

They were so big, though, only two could fit side by side in the tunnel. And as one broke ahead of the other, it came at Ethan down the *middle* of the corridor. It blocked the others behind it.

A lucky break. Kind of.

At least he'd only be squished by one of them.

"Go!" he ordered his team. "I'll stay and slow it down."

"Not by yourself, Ethan," Bobby said, and stood by him.

Emma shot him a *don't be stupid* look and halted as well.

Angel stopped. Her one eye not covered by her angular haircut looked at Ethan and then the robot. She rushed forward, grabbed Emma's plasma torch, and shoved her rivet gun into his sister's hands.

Emma looked at it, not understanding.

Angel didn't explain. She turned and ran, leaving them behind.

Ethan didn't have time to think about her crazy actions, because the first robot was almost on him.

He raised his crowbar again. This was reckless, suicidal, and just as crazy as anything Angel had ever done. That didn't matter.

Emma gritted her teeth and opened fire.

Rivets sparked off the robot's shell. One metal projectile shattered a camera lens.

The robot shook its head, momentarily disoriented . . . but it didn't slow down.

It rolled at Ethan fast, so close now, he smelled the grease from its joints.

Bobby shoved Ethan out of the way—an instant before the robot would've flattened him—and then Bobby chucked his chain at the robot's wheel.

The robot clipped Bobby on the arm, which spun him around.

The chain, though, sucked into the wheel well and wrapped around the axle.

The wheel seized—

And the rest of the robot kept moving forward.

Its body whipped around the immobilized wheel.

It slammed into the floor deck, face-first. The impact drove the robot *through* the deck plates. Its arms, one with a jackhammer still sputtering, bent at right angles. Red hydraulic fluid gushed everywhere.

Behind the mutilated robot, the other mechanized men halted . . . unable to pass over the wreckage. They looked back and forth and murmured chirps of static. They then started to cut and hammer apart their still-struggling teammate to get past.

Ethan blinked at the horrifying sight. He got to his feet.

Bobby's left arm hung at an unnatural angle, clearly broken, but he was grinning from ear to ear.

"Come on," Emma urged. "That bought us maybe a minute."

She ran down corridor G-422.

Ethan and Bobby chased after her. Bobby's busted arm slowed him down, and he grunted from the pain every time it moved.

Ahead on the wall were sparks and snaps of an intense white light. Ethan squinted and made out the shadowy outline of Angel, kneeling with the plasma torch by one of those stuck submarine-like doors.

With a *clang* the door's lockbox dropped to the

floor. Angel yanked the door. It squealed on its hinges and opened about a foot. She didn't wait for the others. She slipped inside.

Emma was right behind her. Ethan shoved Bobby through and then followed.

It was dark. There were no echoes like out in the tunnel. The space felt smaller.

Ethan reached for his flashlight but realized he'd dropped it at the intersection. There was no going back for it now.

Angel waved the plasma torch about. Ghostly shadows flickered over the walls near the door. They made her face look more psychotic than usual.

Ethan pulled the door shut . . . or tried to anyway. He strained and used his full weight and it squeaked shut.

Emma then attacked the metal door with the rivet gun, tacking it to its frame.

"That's not going to last long," Ethan said. "Look for another exit. There has to be one in—"

The rest of his words stuck in his throat.

The room was only six paces wide. But it was long. Very long . . . vanishing into the distance. Along the walls were shelves and a series of tracks with tiny dead robots that looked as if they had once rolled up and down the tracks.

The thing that made Ethan pause, though, was what was on the shelves. They were packed with slender crystalline rectangles. Even covered with dust, they still glimmered sapphire blue, ruby red, and clear, sparkling diamond.

These were the same electronic crystal books he had seen at the library in New Taos.

Whoever built Titan Base had stored a treasure trove of ancient knowledge down here.

More important, there had to be a reader for these electronic books nearby. Ethan had checked out a book from New Taos containing information on Project Prometheus. It was connected to his parents and the strange mental abilities he and Emma seemed to have. It might have been the key to unlocking the mystery of why their parents had raised them in Santa Blanca.

He searched the nearest self. There had to be a reader here somewhere.

Angel, however, moved farther down the long room . . . taking their only light with her.

Ethan was about to ask her to hold up, when a robot pounded on the door, making it ring like a gong. Another great *thump* popped a few of the new rivets.

"That didn't take long," Bobby whispered. "They must really want us."

"Go. Go," Ethan said, pushing Bobby ahead.

Emma wrapped Bobby's good arm around her neck and handed Ethan the rivet gun. They trotted as fast as they could.

The pounding on the door increased, as if there were two or three robots on it now.

Ethan paused every dozen steps to cover their escape. He wasn't sure what one rivet gun was going to do against those things.

Ahead, Angel and the lit plasma torch halted.

The room was a dead end. There was a set of elevator doors. Angel pushed the call button.

Ethan, Emma, and Bobby caught up to her.

"Is there power?" Bobby asked, panic creeping into his tone.

Ethan and Emma glanced at each other. There had been sporadic power surges and generators starting up in the subbasements. But if there was power down here, they sure wouldn't be running around in the dark.

Angel kept punching the elevator call button—harder and faster—as if she were a wild animal, clawing at her cage to get out.

At the far end of the library corridor, there came a tremendous clatter as the riveted door fell off its hinges.

Emma touched Angel's shoulder. "Don't," she whispered.

Angel slowly nodded. She bonked her head against the elevator door and stayed there.

Emma took the plasma torch from Angel's grasp and turned to face the long passage.

Ethan swallowed, but his throat was too dry for it to do any good.

He couldn't help it. He pressed the call button, as if the bazillion times Angel had tried weren't enough to prove the thing wasn't working.

Ethan felt something as he touched the button. A connect in his mind. A spark. It was a little like the mental connection he could sometime make with his wasp I.C.E. Like the faint static whisper he'd heard in his head when they were in New Taos.

The button lit. It dinged.

Within the walls, motors stirred to life.

The elevator doors parted. Angel almost fell inside.

They all rushed in after her.

Okay. The doors opened. But did this thing have power enough to work? Or would it take them up and get stuck? Or drop them back down? Ethan didn't trust his luck today. Not that he had a choice.

He and Emma pointed their weapons back down the passage . . . waiting for the doors to shut.

Bobby stabbed the top button marked with a star. Angel punched the DOOR CLOSE button.

At the far end of their light, Ethan could make out a monstrous shadow pulling its way toward them with long arms. It looked like it barely fit.

Angel punched the DOOR CLOSE button with her fist hard enough to dent the panel.

The elevator doors started to ease together . . . slowly . . . squealing and wailing.

The robot must have seen, because it pulled its way faster up the passage, wrecking the shelves, crushing crystal books under its wheel.

The doors shut.

The elevator car jerked up.

Ethan stood motionless. Not yet quite believing he was alive. Heart pounding.

"Emma? Ethan? Come in," Felix's voice came over

the radio. "Breaking radio silence as ordered, sir. We found them."

Ethan could move again. He grabbed the radio and clicked open the channel. "We're here," he breathed out with a huge sigh. "Report, Felix."

"We've got Lee and Oliver, sir. They're alive."

"Good," Ethan said. "Everyone—get back up to the Command Center ASAP. Secure all doors behind you. Then weld them shut."

"Sir?" Felix asked.

"We found things, too," Ethan murmured. "And they're also alive."

∘ ∘ ∘ 8 ∘ ∘ ∘

THEY ALMOST GOT US

ETHAN WATCHED SARA TEND TO BOBBY'S ARM.

Bobby, Sara, Ethan, Madison, Lee, and Oliver were in one of the many rooms in the hospital wing of the base. The room had white and blue tiles on the walls and floor. Warm light glowed from fixtures in the corners.

Sara sat next to Bobby on one of the three beds in the room.

Her mother had been a doctor in Santa Blanca, and Sara had volunteered at the hospital after school. Of all of them, she had the only medical training.

Ethan sat on the bed facing Sara and Bobby. Madison

sat on the bed next to him. Not too close. Not too far away either.

Lee and Oliver had parked on the far bed, waiting to be debriefed.

The rest of Sterling Squadron was busy elsewhere. After Ethan described their narrow escape from the robots, they'd all grabbed portable welders and run off to seal every subbasement entrance.

Except Emma—she was in the Command Center to monitor the still-functioning security cameras on base. They had to track those renegade robots.

Bobby winced and cried out as Sara straightened his arm, pulling it from the shoulder joint.

"Hey!" he said.

"You dislocated it," she said. "I had to correctly reposition the bone in the socket. Sorry."

Ethan rubbed his arm in sympathetic pain.

He remembered how Bobby had held on to the chain as he threw it at the robot. When it wrapped about the axle, he'd held on a split second too long and it'd jerked his arm. He was lucky his arm hadn't gotten yanked right *off* his shoulder.

"There," Sara told him as she applied a pain pad on Bobby's shoulder. "That wasn't so bad, was it?"

"Yeah, actually, it was," Bobby said. He smiled, though. "Thanks, Sara."

Bobby and Sara had gone through a lot in Santa Blanca. They found out how the real world worked. Alien invaders. That their parents really didn't love them. They'd formed their own small resistance. They'd survived. And they'd grown close because of it. Ethan could see it in the caring way they looked at each other.

He glanced sideways at Madison.

She caught the look. The corner of her crooked smile quirked at him, but then quickly faded.

What was it that he felt for Madison? They were friends. Wingmates. He trusted her with his life. There was more than that, though.

What had that kiss been all about back in Santa Blanca when she thought she might not ever see him again? Neither of them had mentioned it since they'd been at Titan Base. In fact, Ethan hadn't seen Madison much in the last week. Had they both been too busy? Had she been avoiding him? Or was he avoiding her?

It would have to wait. There were life-and-death serious things that needed Ethan's immediate attention.

"So what happened?" Ethan finally asked Oliver and Lee.

Oliver swallowed hard and backed up on the bed. "Okay," he said. He removed his glasses and closed his eyes. "It started when we left the satellite relay room."

"We'd made the connection and repairs that Emma wanted," Lee added, shaking his head. "It was weird, because as soon as we got the power hooked up down there, all sorts of electrical relays started clicking on . . . by themselves."

"It was like the base had been waiting to wake up or something," Oliver whispered.

The door to the hospital room swished open. Paul and Felix entered.

"Sorry to interrupt, Lieutenant," Felix said. "Paul and I finished sealing section three, and he insisted that we come here."

Paul crossed his arms over his chest. "I want to hear what they have to say, too," he said. "I have a right to know what's going on. It involves us all."

At least Paul was talking to him now. That was progress.

Ethan examined Paul. From Paul's scowling face, Ethan guessed information wasn't the only thing he wanted here. He wanted a showdown.

Well, it was long overdue.

"Fine," Ethan said. He shot Felix a cautioning look. Felix nodded back.

"Go on," Ethan told Lee. "What happened next?"

"We saw something moving in one of those high-voltage electromagnetic relays," Lee said, and his face scrunched up as he forced himself to remember. "It was the size of a mouse. A tiny robot. It sparked and started moving like it had just come to life after being dead for however long this place has been here."

"It repaired the relay," Oliver said.

"After we got over the surprise," Lee said, "we figured it was supposed to be there. Part of the automatic maintenance—"

"Anyway," Oliver interrupted, "we heard you guys over the radio talking about the sortie to help Madison and Angel. We just wanted to get back as fast as we could and help."

Madison blushed at this—embarrassed, angry, or both, Ethan couldn't tell. Ethan knew she'd hated that she and Angel had almost been ambushed by the strange bees and that she hadn't even known they were there.

"So we jogged back," Lee went on, "and that's when we noticed more and more of those little robot guys all over the place."

"Some rolled on one wheel," Oliver added. "Some had four wheels. One was the size of a cat."

"And then," Lee said, "we didn't see any of them for a long time."

"Just two miles of those dark tunnels," Oliver whispered, then shuddered. "Way too creepy."

Everyone in the room shifted uncomfortably, remembering the subbasements. Ethan, too. He could practically smell the rust and feel the smothering press of the stale air and shadows around him.

"Go on," Ethan prompted the boys.

"That's when we heard the big ones," Lee said.

Oliver nodded. "We didn't know exactly what the sounds were. Hammering. Electronic buzzing. Metal being torn. We thought it was more machinery coming on."

"That's when we got back on the radio," Lee said. "When you returned from your fight with the bees."

"And that's when we stumbled into them," Oliver murmured. His dark skin paled.

"We came around a corner into a wide intersection," Lee whispered. "There must've been fifty of the big ones."

"Fifty?" Ethan asked.

Lee and Oliver nodded together.

Bobby had gotten superlucky when he'd dropped *one* (and he'd nearly lost his arm in the process). One intact robot was probably a match for five of them with their improvised weapons.

Fifty? It'd be no contest. The robots would wipe out the entire squadron if they got up there.

"Just like the robots you guys fought in New Taos," Lee said. "Minus the antenna in their hands and the plasma emitters in their heads. They had weapons, though. Crowbars, welders, sonic disruptors, claws."

"They jammed our radio and came straight for us," Oliver said, wringing his hands. "We knew exactly what they wanted to do: tear us apart."

"So we ran," Lee said. He was so agitated now he stood up from the bed. "We zipped into an open area, found an air duct, got in, and crawled away as fast as we could."

"But that didn't stop them," Oliver told them, panic starting to strangle his voice. "They ripped into the ductwork to make it big enough for them to follow!"

"They almost got us, but we jumped across a chasm and got away."

Oliver took a deep breath. "That's it. We found

Felix and Paul"—he gestured at the two boys—"and we got back up here."

Ethan let their story sink in a moment. "Okay," he said. "Thanks. This gives me a lot to think about."

Paul uncrossed his arms. He hesitated, as if he were working up his courage to say something, which was odd, because he'd never had a problem saying what was on his mind before. He exhaled and finally said, "Could I talk to you, Ethan . . . Lieutenant . . . in private?"

He'd tried to make that sound polite—but it still came out sounding like a threat to Ethan.

Of course, it wasn't enough that the Ch'zar were trying to blast him out of the air, and killer robots were on the loose trying to murder him and his squadron . . . now he had to deal with Paul Hicks.

Madison set her hand on Ethan's arm and gave him a tiny warning shake of her head.

Ethan ignored her.

"Let's do this," Ethan said. He stood and motioned for Paul to follow him. "Just you and me. My office."

∘ ∘ ∘ 9 ∘ ∘ ∘

TEST OF COMMAND

ETHAN PUSHED ASIDE THE PAPERWORK ON HIS desk and sat on the edge.

Paul followed him into his office. He shut the door behind him. He didn't come any farther. Instead, he leaned against the closed door, almost as if to hold it shut, so no one else could get in.

"Well?" Ethan demanded.

"Look," Paul said with an apologetic shrug. "I know we've never gotten along. I thought there was a time when, well, never mind. That's not important. We can't do this anymore."

"Do what? Insubordination? Inciting to mutiny?"

"See?" Paul said, and pointed at Ethan. "That's exactly what I'm talking about. You keep *pretending* you're in charge."

Ethan opened his mouth to say something, but no words came.

Pretending he was in charge?

That's not what he was doing, was it?

The others believed in him. They took his orders. They'd followed him into the battle. He knew they trusted his judgment.

Ethan pursed his lips. How did Paul always get him to doubt himself? "I *am* in command here," he said.

"Sure, you're in command," Paul said with a snort. "But is that the right thing? I mean, maybe, before, when you had Irving and Winter calling the strategic shots, you leading a squadron might have made sense. You're pretty good, Blackwood. Maybe even as good as me." Paul smirked, but it quickly vanished. "That's not good enough anymore."

Ethan flushed and felt like he was going to boil over. Maybe it was mentioning Dr. Irving and Colonel Winter so causally after they'd died to give this squadron a chance to live. Maybe it was the fact that Paul Hicks was an idiot.

If Paul had been talking this way to Colonel Winter, she would have called the guards and had Paul thrown in the brig. Forever.

Ethan wasn't the colonel, though. He didn't have any guards. Or a brig.

He took a deep breath and cooled off. "You think someone else needs to lead? You, maybe?"

Paul held up his hands and laughed. "No way. What I'm saying is that maybe *none of us* should be leading."

"Huh?"

"If the Resisters and Seed Bank were around," Paul said, growing serious, "we wouldn't be talking. But there's no more lieutenants or colonels. There's just a few kids trying to stay alive. We should *all* get a say in what we do next. And why not? Every decision could be life and death for all of us."

Ethan blinked.

He hadn't been expecting a rational suggestion from Paul. Another challenge, sure. Maybe even a few punches and some wrestling.

Ethan felt like he'd been punched anyway.

Paul had a point. A democracy made sense.

Who was he to lead them all? Colonel Winter and Dr. Irving had had decades of experience before they'd given orders that affected the fate of every free-willed human left on Earth.

Besides, was he doing such a great job? There was a new Ch'zar I.C.E. out there that had outflown them. There were robots on the loose, trying to disassemble the entire squadron limb from limb.

If they pooled their thinking, if they all had a vote, would they make better choices?

"Look," Paul said. His gaze fell to the floor. "I know things haven't been easy. I even appreciate the job you've done so far. You kept us alive. I'll give you that. But things have changed, Ethan, and not for the better. You have to change, too, or you're going to get us all killed."

Killed.

There it was. Plain and simple.

Was Ethan really arrogant enough to think he had all the answers? He was bound to make some wrong choices. What if that meant dooming the last survivors of the human race?

It was almost impossible to believe that he could do it alone.

He stopped. He'd almost let Paul make him think that.

But Ethan remembered what Dr. Irving had told him before Ethan had gone into battle—Dr. Irving, who had once commanded armies and been called the grand admiral of the air, the Storm Falcon. He'd asked Dr. Irving why he and the colonel had picked him to lead Sterling Squadron. Dr. Irving told Ethan he had *"an incredible aptitude for aerial combat, a strategic genius, and a certain disregard for authority."*

And then there were Colonel Winter's last orders to him: take the squadron, run, and hide. She told him the Resistance would live on through him.

So . . . regardless of what *he* thought about *himself*, the colonel and the doctor, with decades of command experience, had picked Ethan Blackwood to lead.

He hadn't wanted this command. It had nonetheless been given to him.

It was his responsibility, and he wasn't about to give it away.

"What you're talking about won't work," Ethan told Paul. "Not in a crisis situation. Not when we're at war."

Paul looked up. His scowl was back, stretching the scars on his face into ugly white lines.

"Imagine Angel giving orders," Ethan said. "Or some of the newer people who have never been in battle. That's exactly why there is a chain of command in war, because tough, unpopular orders have to be made and carried out. Most times those orders have to be made quickly, without a lot of discussion. That's how we're going to survive. That's how the human race is going to win."

Paul opened his mouth to speak, but Ethan cut him off.

"That's my final decision, Private Hicks. Thank you for your suggestions. You are dismissed."

Ethan heard those words come from him, but they made it sound like it was Colonel Winter speaking.

Paul's mouth shut with a clack of teeth. He turned and left.

Ethan exhaled. He felt like he had passed an important test. Not with flying colors, but something like a C minus.

Command of Titan Base was still his, though. He was going to make it count.

He grabbed his walkie-talkie. "Sergeant Winter," he said. "I need you in my office."

"I'm on my way," Felix said, with a crackle of static.

While he waited for Felix, Ethan read over his last status report. He considered the list of names he was responsible for. It was a terrifyingly short number that made up the very last of the free humans on Earth. He noted (with some difficulty) that Paul's name was there. Paul was Ethan's responsibility, too.

He had to figure out a way to make their small numbers count and turn the situation around.

He couldn't give up.

There came a polite knock at the door, and Felix entered. He must have been nearby to have gotten there so quick.

Felix scanned the empty office. "Hicks is gone?"

"He left. He's one of the things I want to talk to you about, Sergeant. First, though, make sure all the tunnels below level three are sealed. We have the fewest entry points there. I want you to personally inspect every hatch, tunnel, and duct."

"I'm on it," Felix told him.

"Afterward, gather everyone and meet Emma and me in the Command Center. We'll take a long look at what the Ch'zar are up to. Then we'll figure out their plans and throw a few dozen monkey wrenches into them."

"Yes, sir." That got a grin out of Felix. "Now we're talking."

He started to leave.

"Felix," Ethan said. "About Paul . . ."

Felix turned around, and his expression darkened. "He's a great pilot, Ethan. I wish he wasn't such a handful."

"I want you to assign someone we count on to watch him."

Sterling Squadron had enemies coming at them from below. They had enemies above in the Ch'zar—and now the squadron just might have had a third enemy, this time among them.

"I don't trust Paul Hicks anymore," Ethan whispered.

∘ ∘ ∘ 10 ∘ ∘ ∘

INNER TURMOIL

ETHAN LOOKED ACROSS THE CAVERNOUS COM-
mand Center. His attention was not on the dazzling array of 360-degree wall screens, but rather on the people
on the raised stage.

The kids rescued from Santa Blanca clustered together, staring and pointing at the eastern coast of
North America. They'd come so far in the last week—
adjusting to a horrible reality that had nearly driven
Ethan over the edge.

Felix stood close to Emma as she adjusted the display controls. Their arms occasionally brushed against

each other. They looked like a couple at a school dance. He was happy for them. (Although in the back of his mind, Ethan was worried that this potential romance might mean puberty was not far off for those two, which was a *big* problem.)

And speaking of romances . . .

Madison sat on a railing a short way off. She held a digital clipboard and made notes as she squinted at a map sector near Chicago. She puffed the spike of hair that hovered over her face. Today her hair was the color of polished walnut. Ethan suspected this was her real color, and he liked it.

Right now, though, they couldn't be more than friends. He had to give her orders. She was in his squadron, fighting by his side. Complicating that with any boyfriend-girlfriend stuff wouldn't be smart.

The escapees from Sterling Reform School were scattered about the central stage, a little less in awe of the gigantic real-time world maps.

Kristov wasn't there, though.

Felix had ordered him to shadow Paul, who also wasn't there.

Motion in his peripheral vision caught Ethan's attention.

An image of Paul passed in front of a security camera. He was down one level, headed east. Those camera feeds were displayed on the stations near Emma to track any robotic intruders.

A minute later, Kristov showed up in the same passage, far enough behind Paul so he wouldn't be seen.

Ethan sighed, wondering what Paul was up to now. However, he had to focus on the rest of his team.

He clapped his hands together. "Okay, people!" Ethan shouted. "Here's the plan."

Everyone stopped what they were doing and faced Ethan. He felt the mantle of command settle on his shoulders.

"Like Emma said before," Ethan told them, "we need to each take a section of the map and figure out what the Ch'zar are up to. Madison and Angel saw a lot of ground activity in the central part of North America. And we saw those weird bees in the American Southwest. There are none of the usual aerial combat patrols—so the enemy has to be up to *something*. We need to know what, so we can plan our next move."

Lee raised a hand. "What about the robots?" he asked, and pointed at the floor.

"All entrances to the subbasement are sealed," Ethan

said. "We're monitoring all access points on the security feeds. If they try to break through, I'll take an I.C.E. and destroy that section of the base if need be." He smacked his fist into his hand for emphasis.

Lee and Oliver nodded, appreciating the finality of this option as a solution to the robot problem.

"Okay, Emma," Ethan said. "Show us what to do."

Emma took over then. She gave them a tutorial on how to use gestures to zoom in and pull out the satellite's view on sections of the map, how to shift to infrared and ultraviolet spectrums, and how to label objects and even track them over time.

The team drifted to different parts of the huge walls. Ethan gravitated to an isolated spot—the Yucatán Peninsula. Back in his Northside Elementary geography class, he'd learned this was a jungle-covered part of Mexico near the equator.

Madison settled near the wall by Ethan, scanning Mexico City.

He glanced over and saw it wasn't one of the most populated cities in the world as he had been taught, but just a small town, almost identical to Santa Blanca.

How else had the Ch'zar changed the world since they took over?

He returned to his section of the wall, the Yucatán Peninsula. As he'd expected, it was jagged coastlines, sandy beaches, and lush tropical rain forests—that unexpectedly shifted from wilderness to a smoke-belching factory.

He pulled the view back out and found it wasn't a single factory either. Or even a complex of factories. This was an industrial landscape . . . five hundred square miles of toxic lakes, red-hot furnaces, conveyor belts, and oil refineries.

Metal and plastic parts, even disassembled organic I.C.E. limbs, rolled out to freeway-sized conveyor belts and onto trucks with segmented beds and sixteen wheels. A steady stream of these vehicles carted it all off to the south.

"What the heck is this?" he whispered.

Ethan had known the Ch'zar were using Earth's resources to build more spaceships and seed distant worlds, but he had no idea just how big their operation was.

"Here," Madison said. "I've spotted enemy combat I.C.E. locusts. Heading your way."

Ethan reached over and slid the tracking icon she'd attached to the moving unit. He tapped on it and the view zoomed in.

These Shiva-class locust I.C.E.s had mottled purple-and-black exoskeletons, barbed forelimbs, extra heavy armor, hind-leg grenade launchers, and jaws strong enough to rip through steel like papier-mâché.

He shuddered. He'd fought too many of these, and they always scared him. If he was piloting his wasp I.C.E., it would have instinctively tried to blast one of the locusts with its stinger or bite its head off. He blinked, clearing that vision from his mind.

A blur flashed over the image—a flutter of chitinous wings and slashing mandibles.

He twisted the zoom back to better see what was going on.

A locust had landed and battled three black army ants. It easily tore through the smaller ants' armor, biting legs off with its powerful jaws. Five more ants, though, appeared from tunnels. They grabbed the locust and nipped its vulnerable unarmored joints. All five got a good grip on it—tugging and yanking—wrenching the locust's limbs out of its sockets! The limbs twitched and shuddered and leaked ichor, still biting and trying to fight. The ants moved on.

What the heck was going on? Horrified, fascinated, Ethan pulled the camera angle farther back.

Curious, Madison came over to watch.

A dozen locusts fought a hundred army ants, tumbling and wrestling over trucks and crushing conveyor belts in the process. Overhead, yellow-green wasps flew and lanced the ground with laser fire. White beetles launched missiles into the fray—fighting *both* sides!

Felix and several others moved over to watch as the warfare splashed across the wall screens.

"Those are Ch'zar combat I.C.E.s," Felix whispered.

"That doesn't make any sense," Ethan said. "The Ch'zar have one collective mind. They don't fight each other."

"Then they have to be Resisters," Emma replied, and jumped up and down for joy. "Seed Bank survivors like us. They must've stolen those I.C.E.s."

A spark of hope flared inside Ethan. During the last battle for the Seed Bank, he'd seen Jack Figgin's squadron, the Black and Blue Hawks, destroyed. But he was never sure what happened to the other kid pilots, especially Becka's Bombers. Considering the overwhelming odds, he assumed that they were either dead or captured as well. But if anyone could have made it, it would have been Rebecca and her bomber squadron. She was tough and smart.

His hope, however, flickered and then went out as he remembered a technical detail.

"It's not so simple to commandeer Ch'zar I.C.E.s," Ethan said, and turned to Madison. "Isn't that right?"

Madison tapped her lower lip, frowning. "No," she answered. "If there's a human pilot inside, well, I've heard extractions usually require . . . surgery."

"And if they don't have human pilots," Felix added, now glaring at the viewscreen, trying to figure this all out, "there are no cockpits inside. That's why we always had to grow our I.C.E.s from genetically engineered eggs."

Ethan watched the carnage, not knowing what to make of it.

Insects ripping other insects apart. There were fires, explosions, wreckage, and hundreds of twitching bodies littering the industrial landscape.

But it seemed that the army ants had won. They started disassembling factory walls and tearing into the inside.

"This is so weird," Ethan said.

"Ethan!" Oliver cried. He was on the center stage staring at the computer monitors. "Over here. A fight!"

"We know it's a fight," Madison answered him. "We're watching over here, too."

"No," Oliver said, a look of worry and confusion masking his face. "It's Paul."

Ethan's head whipped around as if he'd been slapped. He forgot about the bug warfare and ran to center stage to the security camera monitors.

On the smaller screen, Kristov and Paul circled each other. There was no sound feed. Kristov silently threw a fist at Paul. Paul ducked and planted a head butt into the larger boy's stomach.

Kristov doubled over. Paul jumped on top of him and clubbed the side of Kristov's head with double fists.

Kristov lay there, no longer moving.

Paul slowly got to his feet. He glowered at the security camera overhead and then ran off.

Ethan checked the computer monitor. This particular camera watched the place he feared Paul would've gone.

"The flight deck," Ethan said. "Paul's gone too far this time."

∘ ∘ ∘ 11 ∘ ∘ ∘

CHANGE IN THE LINEUP

ETHAN AND THE OTHERS RAN OUT INTO THE wide-open space of the flight bay. The deck lights were on minimal power so it was hard to make out details, but Ethan couldn't miss their I.C.E.s lined up and readied for takeoff. They were giant forms of shadow . . . and one smaller human figure that darted from insect to insect.

There was a groan to Ethan's right.

Kristov slowly tried to sit up, failed, and rubbed his head.

"Sara," Ethan whispered, "see how bad he's hurt. The rest of you, with me."

Sara stayed back to help Kristov. Ethan quietly jogged toward the I.C.E.s. "Fan out," he murmured to the others. "Don't let him get away."

Felix lingered by the wall, fiddling with some light controls.

The deck lights warmed and they could finally see.

So could Paul. He whirled around and spotted Ethan and the others coming for him. He sprinted for a tunnel entrance that led to the maintenance decks. He would lose them down there among the machinery.

They raced after him. Paul was fast, though, and had a huge head start.

He was going to get away.

Ethan couldn't let that happen. He halted and closed his eyes. He reached out with his mind for his wasp.

There was a connection. A spark.

The wasp turned to face him. Its stinger laser heated in anticipation of combat.

Ethan ordered his I.C.E. to take off, get ahead of Paul, and blast him with a downdraft from its wings. *That* ought to slow him.

With a great buzzing from its crystalline wings, the wasp sprang into the air. It zipped across the flight bay and hovered in front of Paul.

Paul stopped dead in his tracks, and the color drained from his face. This Ethan saw up close through his mental connection with the wasp.

Instead of buffeting Paul as ordered, though, the wasp lashed out menacingly with its barbed forelimbs.

It missed. On purpose. It was playing before it moved in for the kill.

Ethan could barely hold it back.

He felt the red-hot desire to pounce on this little morsel. Rend Paul into mincemeat. And then eat him.

While Ethan was horrified, he also felt the same impulse to do violence heat within him. Maybe the secret desire to hurt Paul had been in his brain all this time . . . and the wasp was just bringing it to the surface.

No. He wouldn't let the wasp rampage out of control.

He took a deep breath and reasserted command over the insect brain.

The wasp shook its head once and gave in. It angled its wings and buzzed them hard—blasting Paul with a hurricane-force wind.

Paul fell back onto his butt.

The wasp settled onto the deck in front of him with a tremendous *thud*.

Paul scooted back fast.

By then, the others had caught up to Paul, Madison leading the charge.

Paul started to rise, but Madison socked him on the chin, and he went down.

Emma pulled Madison back before she leaped on Paul.

Surrounded by an unfriendly crowd, Paul had the good sense to stay down.

Ethan jogged up to them. He gave a mental push to his wasp. The gigantic creature backed off and relaxed its combative stance.

Paul rubbed his chin and glared at Madison, Ethan, and the wasp. "You," he said with a scowl. "What are you trying to do? Kill me?"

He sounded as if he *wasn't* in trouble. This was Paul's special trick: complete defiance in the face of authority. Ethan had seen him try it before.

But it hadn't worked on Colonel Winter. It wasn't going to work on him either.

"So . . . ," Paul continued, acting like this was still a

huge misunderstanding. "I was just going to run a maintenance routine on my mantis."

"Was that before or after you assaulted Kristov?" Madison demanded.

"That?" Paul smiled. "He just grabbed me, tried to clobber me."

Ethan didn't believe that. They'd all seen Paul on top of Kristov on the security camera. They were both well away from the mantis I.C.E.

Kristov got to his feet with Sara's help, and he marched over. He stood over Paul, his massive fists clenching and unclenching, then relaxed a notch and turned to Ethan. "He was working on his I.C.E., running the preflight checklist. When I asked him what he thought he was doing, he ran. I tried to grab him, but he was too fast. I chased him, but he turned and"—Kristov rubbed his stomach—"he surprised me."

"What *were* you doing with the mantis, Paul?" Ethan asked.

"Just . . ." Paul shut his mouth, then said with a snort, "Whatever. You guys wouldn't believe me."

"Try me."

Paul glared at Ethan, seemed to decide something, and then shook his head.

Angel stepped up and stared down at Paul. She and Paul had gotten along before, but Angel stopped chewing her gum as she examined him, her expression unreadable.

"Well, until you cough up an explanation," Ethan told him, his tone frosty, "you're not flying any I.C.E. under my command."

The ever-present bravado on Paul's features melted away. "You c-can't ground me. You need every pilot, Blackwood. You need me and my mantis."

Ethan had always known there was something wrong with Paul—he was arrogant and a total pain. But he always thought he could count on Paul in a fight. Now? He wasn't convinced Paul hadn't been trying to steal the mantis . . . to do what? Leave? Paul wouldn't survive without the squad and this base.

The bottom line, though, was Ethan wasn't sure what Paul had planned, but he *was* sure he didn't trust Paul anymore.

Paul stared up at Ethan, unbelieving. "Y-you need me."

"I did need you," Ethan said. "But you crossed the line when you attacked Kristov. Until you can explain your actions, I consider you a danger to the rest of the squad."

Ethan turned to Felix. "Sergeant, you and Kristov stick him in one of the hospital rooms and spot-weld the air vents and door. We'll have a long talk with him when we get back."

Felix nodded and hauled Paul to his feet.

Paul sagged, defeated, shook his head, and muttered, "You'll see. You're going to need me yet, Ethan."

Ethan watched him go. He had a sick feeling in the pit of his stomach.

Emma moved to Ethan's side. "You did the right thing," she whispered. "Or maybe you should have gagged him as well, I dunno."

"Thanks," he whispered back, and then so softly only he heard, "I *hope* I did the right thing."

Madison flashed her green eyes at the looming wasp. "It freaks me out how you can do that." She gave a half shudder. "You just said *'when we get back,'* Lieutenant? Where are we going? What's the plan?"

Ethan stood straighter and spoke up so everyone could hear. "We're flying south to the Yucatán Peninsula. The Ch'zar are fighting each other down there. We're going to find out why. Maybe help them destroy each other."

Everyone nodded.

"And the praying mantis?" Angel asked. She brushed her hair back and looked at the Sterling pilots.

That problem, at least, Ethan had an answer for. He turned to Bobby.

"Bobby," he said. "Front and center."

Bobby ran up to Ethan and saluted.

"You've logged more simulator hours in an I.C.E. than any other new recruit. I think you're ready for your maiden flight."

Bobby looked superserious. "Yes, sir!" he said. "Absolutely!"

Ethan took Bobby's hand and shook it. "Welcome to the squadron, Private Buckman. The Crusher is yours."

Bobby glanced over at the ghostly green praying mantis sitting on the flight deck. The unit looked terrifying just sitting there inert. He swallowed, and whispered, "Yes, sir."

∘ ∘ ∘ 12 ∘ ∘ ∘

CANNIBALIZING

ETHAN SAT INSIDE THE COCKPIT OF HIS WASP, contoured seat hugging his back, hurtling over a green landscape at a dizzying, terrain-hugging three hundred feet.

He checked his fuel gauge for the tenth time in the last half hour.

Two-thirds full. Not ideal, but good enough.

Half was their turn-around point. It didn't leave much extra for exploration . . . or combat.

He scanned the displays, port and starboard, fore and aft. His sprits rose.

Sterling Squadron was back in the air where they belonged. Madison had the point position in their formation with her dragonfly. The insect glimmered like an emerald in the sunlight. Felix had the rearguard station. His Big Blue rhinoceros beetle was the team's anchor. Next to Felix flew Emma in her four-ton ladybug of death.

Angel's black stealth wasp and Lee's housefly orbited the group—zipping back and forth, up and down, always on the lookout for danger. Oliver's sleek, tough silver cockroach and Kristov's bloodred locust were on either side of Ethan's wingtips.

The Crusher praying mantis rocketed along on the dorsal, or top, side of the formation. That gave Bobby the clearest view of the squadron, and made for the easiest maneuvering.

The mantis I.C.E. was Bobby's now. He was doing good, but considering their speed and the fact that they were on average only separated by a body length, being only *good* could have serious consequences.

He wasn't sure how Bobby would do in a real dogfight.

Ethan paused in his thoughts to consider how the word *dogfight* didn't really apply when he was flying a three-ton insect.

At least up there, Ethan was with people he trusted, and things up in the air were clear-cut. When your enemies wanted to destroy you, you knew. You fought back.

Of course, there were complications, even up there. Like: those mysterious unarmed bees they'd run into yesterday. Why the Ch'zar were apparently attacking their own factories. And—Ethan checked his fuel gauges again—the matter of the extra tanks.

In order to make it all the way to the Yucatán Peninsula in one go, they'd had to attach extra fuel tanks on the I.C.E.s. One was the size of his wasp's abdomen. It was worse for Emma and Felix and their fuel-guzzling, heavily armored assault units. They'd burn through *three* extra tanks . . . two of which had been stashed on the route back.

With a hundred miles still to go, they had to keep them until they were nearly at the Ch'zar industrial sector.

Ethan was itching to get rid of the tanks, though. With the extra weight, maneuvering the wasp felt like flying though syrup, the controls were so sluggish.

And combat? Forget it. With the tanks on, they'd be toast.

"We're almost there," Emma said to him over a private, short-range radio channel. "Stop worrying about the extra weight. You should worry about what happens if one of us catches a stray laser beam or plasma bolt. *Boom!* We're basically flying bombs, you know. . . ." She laughed.

"Ha-ha," Ethan said. "Not funny, Emma."

"Hey—just a reality check," she said.

Ethan glanced back at her ladybug. She was right. One hit on these fuel tanks and they could all go up in a huge chain-reaction fireball.

A line of hills passed under their I.C.E.s as they flew over . . . and the jungle started to change. There were a few tracks cutting through the green dirt roads, a paved highway, and all traces of rainforest vanished—replaced by corrugated steel warehouses, churning factories, and an endless automatic conveyor system shuttling cargo.

"Go short-range encryption," Ethan said, after setting the squadron's radio channel to the low-power secret setting. This would reduce the risk of any enemy listening in.

"What is out here that the Ch'zar would build all this?" Bobby asked.

"There's literally tons of lumber," Emma offered.

"The Ch'zar don't need *wood*," Angel said. "Glance over at two o'clock, toward the sea."

Ethan dialed up the magnification of his cockpit screen in that direction. There were the waves and whitecaps of the Gulf of Mexico . . . but there was also the edge of a crazily huge retaining wall that looked like *ten* Hoover Dams put together.

He probably hadn't seen it from the satellite view before because he was looking straight down the thing. And to be truthful, he hadn't been looking for a mile-long wall holding back a million tons of seawater.

Spiraling around on the dry side of this structure were roads and a hundred cranes and one of the deepest open pits Ethan had ever seen. It had to be some sort of mining operation.

"What are they looking for there?" Felix asked.

"Iridium and nickel," Angel told them over the radio. "Platinum, too. Basically a bunch of rare metals. A long time ago, this giant meteor fell to Earth here. It was full of those metals. It also supposedly contributed to the extinction of the Cretaceous-era dinosaurs."

Ethan flew on for a few heartbeats, flabbergasted.

Angel was the last person he'd expect to know that

stuff. How to light a trash can on fire? She was the person he'd ask. History and geology? No way.

"How do you know that?" Madison asked accusingly.

"I went to school," Angel told her. "I studied. Duh!"

An explosion lit the horizon about five miles away. A pillar of flame rose into the sky, then diminished, and left a curling column of black smoke.

"Okay, people," Ethan snapped. "Cut the chatter. We've got trouble."

"More than you think, Lieutenant," Madison said. "Incoming hostiles, high-speed inbound from nine o'clock. Seventy-five miles out."

At the edge of Ethan's radar screens contacts just appeared. A formation of a dozen Lance-class, hybrid-assault hornets.

Ethan glowered. They were tough fighters.

He quickly assessed the tactical options. Going down, they would find some cover. Probably too late to hide, though.

Ethan almost let go of his control and smacked his head. He was such an idiot!

"Disperse thirty feet and drop your tanks," Ethan ordered the squadron. "Right now!"

He flipped the safety switch on the extra fuel tanks and engaged the PURGE icon.

The extra tank jettisoned and dropped away.

Eight tanks hit the ground. They crushed warehouses and flattened trucks . . . and not a single one of the tanks detonated.

Ethan guessed they were a lot safer than he'd imagined.

Eight? Wait, there were nine of them up there.

A moment later the last tank dropped. Angel's wasp flashed its laser. A spot on her still-airborne tank turned molten.

It blew up just before impact . . . transforming in the blink of an eye into a huge ball of fire, and flattening three nearby warehouses.

That was a nice shot. Ethan was impressed with the destruction. The fuel must have flash-vaporized, somehow making a much bigger bang than he'd ever expect.

He was, though, going to have a long chat (again) with Angel about firing without orders.

"Move up to fifteen thousand feet," Ethan ordered. "We'll try to take the high ground in this fight."

The squadron angled their jets down, and they rose straight up into the air. There was no cloud cover today.

That was good: they'd see anything coming at them. It was also bad: there'd be no cover up there once the shooting started.

Adrenaline surged through Ethan's body. He shook a little. It was a familiar sensation. He also felt the wasp, eager to get to the action, blast with its laser, and tear the enemy apart.

He held them both back . . . experienced enough to know that the fighting would come to them. And when it did, they'd have an advantage being higher.

His displays lit with warning indicators as the hornets' plasma emitters heated. Those Lance-class I.C.E.s packed a wallop.

"Try to save your afterburners," he said over the radio. "We don't have the fuel to burn. Concentrate laser fire on the leads, and then when they . . ."

His voice trailed off.

The hornets were *not* lining up for an attack run. They kept flying straight at the same elevation. It was almost as if they hadn't seen Sterling Squadron in their way.

"Stand by," Ethan said. "No one, and I mean *no* one, open fire until I give the order."

Angel's black wasp zipped in a little anxious circle, but otherwise stayed hovering where she was supposed to.

Ethan watched, fascinated, as the hornets passed right under them . . . and kept going.

They did open fire—but at the ground.

A warehouse the size of a city block erupted into flames. The plasma splashed over the metal and heated it and melted huge gaping holes in the roof.

From the far side of the building, the walls burst open and six Leviathan superheavy assault scarab beetles took to the air. The fat insects banked, their golden armor separated, and missile pods popped open.

The hornets focused plasma fire on the starboard side of the scarabs' formation. One of the beetles ignited like a magnesium flare and dropped to the ground.

The remainder of the scarabs fired. Their missiles detonated and wiped out half of the hornets in a flash of highly explosive thunder that left chitin armor fluttering in the air like confetti.

"Go winged flight," Ethan told his squadron.

Their jets throttled down to a dull roar, cut out, and were replaced by the drone of insect wings.

"Move to three o'clock and increase altitude a thousand feet," he advised, and slowly edged from the battle, still watching the carnage.

"More hornets inbound fast," Madison advised.

In response to this new threat, ant lion artillery unburied themselves from the ground, and the silver armored I.C.E.s launched salvos of anti-aircraft shells into the sky. The air was dotted with smoke puffs and deadly shrapnel.

But they were still taking no notice of Sterling Squadron. It was as if they were referees in this fight. It made no sense.

The hornets were more agile than the scarabs and ant lions. They could make short work of their enemy . . . if they could only get closer. But the beetles and ant lions were effectively using missiles and artillery to create a quarter-mile kill zone.

"Keep moving slowly," Ethan whispered. "Let's not get caught up in this . . . but see if you can find out what they're fighting about. There has to be something here."

Felix maneuvered his rhinoceros beetle closer to Angel's wasp. She behaved, though, and moved off with the rest of them instead of engaging the Ch'zar.

Even ever-ready-for-a-fight Angel wasn't crazy enough to dive into *that* mess.

So just why were they killing each other? Was there a clue here?

Ethan squinted. There were factories and refineries down there, trucks that had been lined up and were now scattered like toys ready to take cargo somewhere. Their fighting over a place and resources they already had made no sense.

His sister's ladybug lagged behind and drifted out of the squadron's formation.

He opened a private radio frequency to her. "Em?"

There was silence over the channel for three heartbeats, then she whispered, "Shhh, Ethan. Listen."

He listened intently over the radio. There was static. His own pulse. Nothing else.

"Not like that," Emma said. "Listen with your mind. To *them*."

Shocked by the suggestion, he pulled back from the speaker.

"No way, Emma. I did that once in combat," he said. "And the ant lion trying to eat us almost blasted a hole in my brain. I'd never try it with so many angry Ch'zar so close."

"You don't understand," she said. "That's the *exact* reason why it does work. They're all focused on each other."

That made zero sense. The Collective didn't focus on itself. It just was. A being composed of millions of minds.

Emma was silent.

Ethan gave in and slowly opened his thoughts a bit . . . and heard nothing, so he opened his mind a bit more. Okay, there was his wasp's mind, agitated they weren't down there in the fight. That was expected.

Farther out he could hear the faint mental echoes of the alien Collective . . . but it was different than he'd remembered it. It wasn't one thundering unified beat. There were *two* songs.

"You hear the different rhythms?" she asked.

"Yes. One's accelerating into a full drumroll. The other is pounding deeper notes. It's almost like they're fighting each other, but in their minds."

"No," Emma corrected. "It's like they're trying to *kill* each other even in their minds."

Below, fires raged. Hornet carcasses burned among wrecked machinery.

"They're not trying," he whispered. "They're doing it."

He spotted movement: one wounded ant lion leaking ichor dragged one of the cargo trucks in its massive jaws. There was another ant lion doing the same thing. They moved away from the battle.

"They're after *stuff*?" he said. "Since when have the Ch'zar been interested in material goods?"

"Ethan?" Felix broke in over the squadron radio channel. "Any further orders, Lieutenant?"

Tension strained Felix's voice. This had to be nerve-racking for the team. Just watching others fight. But they had to gather intelligence on what the enemy was doing. Rushing in now would be the wrong move.

"Let's go higher," Ethan said. "We're going to follow those ant lions hauling materials south."

"Roger that," Felix said.

The squadron pulled into a flying wedge formation and shadowed the insects on the ground.

More ant lions, then black army ants, and even locusts joined the line moving south. They dragged and hauled cargo trucks, and in one case, a dozen ants worked together to pull along a huge industrial pump the size of a house.

They formed a column, a parade, and then a superhighway of giant insects.

Where were they taking all this stuff?

Ethan scanned the landscape from horizon to horizon. The day was bright and sunny. To the south, the factories vanished, and although there were roads, it was mostly jungle. The air was misty, probably a side effect of the lush, wet environment.

Then he saw it: a line that ran from Earth up to the sky. It went up and up until it faded and vanished in the distance . . . even on his display's extreme magnification.

"That's the Ch'zar's equatorial orbital beanstalk," Madison announced over the radio. "It's kind of a long elevator they use to get stuff to their mothership in space."

Ethan marveled at the size and engineering. He'd seen one beanstalk near Santa Blanca the first night he learned the truth. That one had been much, much smaller.

It was, though, where the mass of insects cannibalizing their own factories was headed.

As he tried to puzzle this out there was a flash of silver in Ethan's peripheral vision.

He checked all his monitors. Nothing.

Still, he hadn't imagined it. He had seen something . . .

where there should have been nothing out there with them at two thousand feet.

He looked again, forcing himself not to blink.

There. Almost completely blended into the sky: it was one of those weird bees they'd encountered before.

This one perfectly mirrored their flight path.

Sneaky little creep!

As Ethan kept looking he saw there wasn't one . . . but two . . . and then five . . . and then a dozen of the enemy craft out there, following them three hundred feet off his port wingtip.

° ° ° 13 ° ° °

AMBUSHED ANYWAY

ETHAN DIDN'T MOVE. NOT A MUSCLE. NOT A twitch.

Those bees had outsmarted and outflown him and Sterling Squadron last time . . . and here they'd snuck right up next to his team, and they hadn't even noticed! If it hadn't been for a lucky odd reflection, he'd still be flying clueless.

Okay. He took a deep breath.

It wasn't as if these bees could read his mind. They didn't have X-ray vision to see into Ethan's cockpit and figure out what his next move was going to be.

They were I.C.E.s—supercamouflaged and using some new technologies—but armor plates, flesh and blood, and just as destructible as any other bug.

Once he figured out how to fight them, that was.

On a hunch, Ethan switched his displays to the infrared spectrum. There were a couple of faint red smudges, but no jet exhaust signatures from those bees. Their jets weren't deployed.

That could give Ethan an advantage, assuming his squadron's jet fuel held out.

He tapped his screen twice to call up the drawing pallet. He drew a circle around the nearest bee, then the others he could make out. He wrote in block letters next to the circled bees: WAIT.

Ethan gave the "go silent" command over the squadron channel and then transmitted a picture of what was on his screen.

He hoped Angel and the others kept their cool, waiting for his lead, and didn't start blasting away!

He held his breath.

Good. They all stayed flying in formation as if nothing was going on.

Seven radio clicks returned, signaling that his team had indeed received his nonverbal message and understood.

Ethan considered his options. The best seemed to be action. Ambush these ambushers!

On-screen he circled the closest bee a few times and then the next closest pair. He numbered them and wrote:

> Concentrate laser fire on number 1.
> Take it out first.
> Then 2 and 3.
> Wait for me!

He sent that over the short-range encrypted squadron channel.

They'd only get one shot to take out as many bees as possible before they scattered. After that it was going to be tricky to pick them out again from the surrounding sky.

He slowly heated his laser to combat readiness.

Inside his gloves his palms were slick with sweat.

He gripped the controls tighter and snapped the wasp's wings forward to turn and blast the enemy with his laser.

The bees darted out of his line of fire—moving a split second before he'd committed to battle.

Ethan didn't have a clear shot. He fired anyway. The laser missed the bee's abdomen, but grazed one of its trailing legs.

That wouldn't slow the thing down. It did, though, heat the exoskeleton by a few hundred degrees and make it flare on his infrared thermal display like a slice of sunshine against the sky.

"Where'd they all go?" Bobby cried over the radio.

Ethan spared a split-second glance. The other bees were gone. They were so well camouflaged they might as well have been invisible.

Except for the one Ethan had tagged with his laser.

He could still see it, for now, but it was cooling, getting dimmer on his infrared display even as he watched.

"Come on," he said. "Turn on your thermals. You can see one. Follow me—quick."

He chased after the enemy bug.

And *again* it guessed his maneuver, and barrel-rolled in the other direction.

How did they know? This guy was good.

Ethan rolled into an inverted dive. He used his jets. The acceleration crushed him into his seat. He banked into the correct angle to catch the bee. The distance between them was closing fast.

On his rear-facing displays, though, Ethan saw that he'd left the rest of his squadron behind as they oriented and turned to catch up. It would take a few seconds for them to get to where he was. And a few seconds in aerial combat could make all the difference.

He couldn't wait for them. He had to go for it.

Part of him knew this wasn't the smartest thing to do.

On the other hand, wasn't it just as stupid *not* to take advantage of his luck? Nab this nearly invisible enemy while he could see it?

The thing's fading thermal glow was almost at ground level now. Ethan rocketed after it.

The bee was so low it brushed the tree line. Branches and leaves flew into the wasp, bouncing harmlessly off, but Ethan almost instinctively yanked up on the controls . . . which would've given that thing more maneuvering room.

It was exactly what he would have done in its place.

The bee swayed and rolled back and forth, so Ethan couldn't get a weapon's lock. He opened fire anyway, hoping for another lucky strike.

The laser missed, but Ethan kept firing wildly. He hit the trees and set them on fire.

His laser then sliced across one of the bee's wings, right at the shoulder joint, and it smoldered.

The wing seized.

The bee plummeted into the jungle.

Trees shattered into matchstick kindle.

"Yes!" Ethan cried. "Gotcha."

"Hey," Emma called over a private radio frequency. "Wait for us, hothead. I mean, Lieutenant. We lost the rest of those bees. They could be anywhere."

But Ethan ignored his sister and banked hard, circled back, and landed . . . Or rather he was going to land, but there could be no landing where the bee had crashed.

There was a huge sinkhole whose edges were tangled with vines and clinging trees. It was three hundred feet across.

Ethan couldn't see the bee or its heat signature down in the pit.

He scanned the nearby jungle. The impact trail of the bee had shattered trees and left skid marks right to and over the edge of the hole. The enemy I.C.E. had to be down there.

He should wait for the others. But he just knew if the bee was still alive, it was thinking of a way to outsmart him once again. He had to make sure it was out of the fight.

"Watch the airspace over me," he ordered on the squadron channel. "The enemy might have doubled back and still be flying. Watch for the faint thermal on the infrareds. Felix, Bobby, follow me down when you catch up."

"Roger that," Felix replied.

Ethan plunged into the sinkhole.

Thorny vines and flowering orchids covered the walls. The plants stopped a hundred feet down, though, as shadows swallowed everything. Bats whirled around him, startled.

Ethan hit his external lights and played them along the walls. They were limestone, cream and rust-colored and melted from a century of erosion.

Four hundred feet and the wasp touched the sinkhole's floor. A small river only a few feet deep ran across the cavern. There were three tunnels with streams that fed the larger river. Mist curled up into the air.

There was an obvious impact crater, and a dragging trail across wet sand into one of the tunnels.

So, that bee *was* down there. It couldn't have gotten far. He had it.

Which was exactly when ice water filled Ethan's veins . . . because he realized that the darkness around him was moving. Faint blue and white smudges circled him, which were easier to see now against the pure black.

He was surrounded by the entire enemy I.C.E. bee squadron.

○ ○ ○ 14 ○ ○ ○

WRESTLING

ETHAN FROZE.

His wasp didn't. White-hot anger flared in its insect brain. It knew exactly what to do.

Ethan let his mind connect deeper with the wasp's and they moved as one—

Pouncing on the closest bee. The wasp pinned the bee, forelimbs to forelimbs, legs to legs.

Camouflaged or not, the bee was still there, solid enough for the wasp to bite at the exposed wings. He tore one of the diamond-hard surfaces from its motorized gimbal with a sparking screech.

The bee struggled and buzzed, but there was no way Ethan and the wasp were letting it get away.

The rest of the bees had other ideas.

They all jumped on the wasp, pulled and tugged and yanked until *its* limbs were stretched wide. They nipped at the unarmored joints.

Fire lanced through Ethan's arms and legs, pain flashing though the wasp's mental connection.

He screamed. Not in fear. He and the wasp were shouting in rage.

The wasp snapped out with its jaws biting back—caught one of the bees' legs and snipped it off.

Two of the bees actually backed off.

Ethan shook off the wasp's blood rage.

Ch'zar didn't do that. They weren't afraid to be hurt or die.

And why was he so angry at them? For some reason this didn't feel like fighting Ch'zar. If felt . . . it kind of felt like the worst time he and Emma had fought. Like it was personal. But that was crazy. Why would he feel like that?

The ground shuddered. Dirt rained down the sink-hole walls.

What now? Ant lions? Scorpions?

A huge blue-black shape emerged from the darkness and mist. It was Felix's rhinoceros beetle. Next to him was the ghost-green praying mantis. Bobby.

Ethan grinned.

Now this was a fight.

Blue plasma heated and sparked between the rhinoceros beetle's horned antennae.

"Hold it, Felix," Ethan cried out over the radio. "In this tight space, you'll roast us all. Go hand to hand, guys."

"With pleasure," Bobby replied.

The bees moved, reacting a second before the Resisters.

The three pinning Ethan's wasp stayed and started pulling him apart once more. The other bees closed in on Bobby and Felix.

It was as if these bees were listening in to Ethan's encrypted radio transmission. It was a code the Ch'zar had never cracked before . . . but what if the Ch'zar had nabbed a survivor from the Seed Bank and knew everything they knew? Who could've survived the explosion that had destroyed the old Resister base? It'd leveled the entire mountain.

More pressing questions had to be answered first,

though. Like: how was Ethan going to stop these bees from dismembering his wasp?

His insect's limbs creaked from the stress. His right forelimb pinged and popped. The hydraulic pressure inside was at the red line as Ethan tried to pull back. His forelimb was either going to be yanked out of the socket—or explode from the inside out!

He fired his laser, a continuous beam that drained his reserve energies, whipping the wasp's stinger wildly.

The temperature in the cave jumped. Old vines that had fallen on the ground ignited. Flickering firelight made the rock walls look like the inside of a volcano.

On Ethan's thermal imagers everything was tinged red.

The laser struck one bee in the head. It released the wasp, shaking its head, stunned.

Ethan had room to maneuver now. He pushed one bee off him so hard it slid on its back across the cavern.

He slammed the remaining bee on him into the wall.

Chunks of limestone fell around them. The bee was stuck tight in a bee-sized hole in the wall. It buzzed, helpless.

Meanwhile, Felix wrestled with a number of bees.

They piled onto the massive beetle. He shook them off like a dog shaking off water droplets after a bath. Bobby in his mantis tried to engage in hand to hand (or in this case, claw to claw) combat. He should have torn the smaller, weaker bees to shreds with the Crusher praying mantis, but because he'd never fought in an I.C.E. for real before, he was barely able to shove his opponents away.

Ethan had to help Felix and Bobby, but first, he'd deal with that other bee on him.

He turned to track the bee he'd pushed. It was on its feet and warily approaching him. Through the heat haze, Ethan noticed that one of its hind legs glowed slightly hotter than the others.

Was this the bee he'd hit first with his laser? The one that had lured him into this trap?

The anger he'd felt before came rushing back. But this time, it wasn't the wasp's insect rage . . . it was all Ethan.

Ethan lunged forward, launching in the air, and dive-tackled the bee.

They tumbled over and over, crashing through the wall and into a side tunnel. The wasp lashed out with its stinger, skewering one of the bee's legs. Too bad there was no energy left in the laser, or he could've fried the thing from the inside out.

The bee struck back. It scraped at the wasp's main external camera, catching, and pulled the lens off. Ethan's central viewscreen burst into static.

The wasp head-butted the bee and clamped its right forelimb in its jaws.

The bee buzzed like an alarm clock and struggled, wiggling so fast that Ethan couldn't clamp his wasp's jaws hard enough to sever the limb.

The bee furiously scrambled against the wasp's abdomen, at a tiny section of its armor.

Ethan heard a pop down there. An armor plate? Unlikely. And even if it was armor, there were no vital systems down there.

He focused instead on curling his stinger around so he could thrust it into the bee's heart.

The bee pushed—and they went tumbling in a deadly embrace, back and forth . . . until Ethan slammed the bee up against a rock wall. It was a good pin.

This thing was as good as dead.

The strange thing was, though, that the bee kept digging at the wasp's abdomen . . . that one spot just to one side.

What was it trying to do? Tickle the wasp?

It didn't matter. Ethan had the bee. Just about. One little shove and he'd have it in the right position to skewer it with the wasp's stinger.

Ethan felt a heaviness in the wasp's limbs. They grew sluggish.

He jiggled the controls, but it was like there was concrete hardening around the I.C.E. . . . and then it froze.

The wasp's brain raged against this new restraining force. It couldn't budge!

Had the bee stung *him* first? Some paralyzing toxin?

Ethan doubted it. He had the bee pinned. The enemy I.C.E. was as immobilized as his wasp.

The two giant insects glared at each other with unblinking eyes.

Ethan gulped.

Had it been able to sneak in a sting? That scraping on his wasp's abdomen . . .

Ethan turned his starboard camera down to that spot. There was indeed an armor plate the size of Ethan's hand missing. No, actually it was hinged. It was still there, just swung open.

Ethan recognized it. It was an access port for the

I.C.E.'s hydraulic fluid regulator. It had a supertricky catch, so complicated that even Ethan had never bothered with it. He'd always left it to the Seed Bank technicians.

It was open now, though.

Ethan angled his camera for a better view. To his horror he saw that a loop of hydraulic line had been pulled out—and severed. Red hydraulic fluid had gushed onto the dirt floor . . . there was only a dribble left coming out.

In a panic, Ethan checked his hydraulic pressure. Almost zero.

How had that thing known just where to disable the one system that'd lock the wasp's limbs? Even Ethan wouldn't have thought of that.

He reached for the radio to call Felix—and halted.

If these bees could overhear their transmissions like he suspected, he was just as likely to alert the nearby Ch'zar I.C.E.s in the jungle with a distress call.

He couldn't wait. He had to get out while there was some pressure left in the hydraulics.

"Sorry," he whispered to the wasp.

He felt a momentary stab of guilt for abandoning his I.C.E., but Ethan nonetheless hit the emergency hatch release, and with the last little bit of hydraulic power (and a good shove from Ethan) the cockpit eased open.

Ethan dropped from the wasp and looked around the tunnel, wary of any approaching enemy I.C.E.s. He was toast if they caught him out in the open.

There was also the pinned bee to consider.

He had to get at *its* hydraulics, like it had done to him—before it got free.

He worked up his courage and took a step toward the two-ton bee.

Its cockpit opened.

Ethan instinctively raised his hands, ready to fight. All his combat training in the Resisters came rushing back . . . which he then promptly forgot.

He dropped his guard.

A girl clambered out of the bee.

It was Rebecca Mills, commander of Becka's Bombers.

∘ ∘ ∘ 15 ∘ ∘ ∘

STANDOFF

ETHAN FACED REBECCA.

And it *was* Rebecca Mills. No one else had a shaved head with such superclose, precise lines on her neck and temples (not even Felix). No other girl he'd ever known had had flaming red hair like hers or a scar that ran from her chin, across her lips, to the tip of her nose either. She had such an intense glare she could've stared down Madison.

Ethan's hands rose once more, balling into fists.

And there was no way Rebecca Mills could be here, except for one way: she was Ch'zar.

Ethan was only alive and here and himself because he'd had the absurd luck of having his parents' letters that led him along a trail of clues to find Titan Base.

Rebecca and her crew, even if they'd had supplies, couldn't have swapped their bumblebee bomber I.C.E.s for new ones and made it all the way to Central Mexico without being . . .

"Ch'zar . . . ," they said together.

She inched closer.

This explained, at least, how the Ch'zar had known all his moves and outfoxed him in the air. Rebecca had helped give Ethan his flight training.

Ethan stepped back—just in time to miss her right cross as her fist came speeding at his jaw. She followed up with a kick that *didn't* miss his stomach.

All the air gushed out of his body, and he doubled over . . . but not before he connected his fist with her nose.

Rebecca staggered back. She shook her head, and droplets of blood went flying from her nose.

She snorted out red-streaked mucus. "I'm sorry they got you, Blackwood. You were the best of us. I thought you'd be the last to go."

"Go? *Me?*" Ethan rubbed the ache out of his gut.

"I didn't go anywhere, thank you very much, Rebecca. *You're* the one they got."

"I don't think so," she growled.

They glared at each other for three heartbeats. Rebecca's laser-intense stare bore into him. Ethan looked her over, searching for a telltale sign . . . of what? That she was still human? Or that she was part of the Ch'zar?

But how did you prove you weren't part of the Ch'zar Collective? Or the better question: how could you prove you were still all human?

It wasn't like they handed out membership cards.

The sounds of combat—multi-ton insect scraping over multi-ton insect, crushing rock, and screeching metal—echoed through the tunnel.

Ethan and Rebecca looked worriedly around.

Felix and Bobby were still out there, fighting for their lives. He and Rebecca couldn't just stand around and argue.

"So prove it," Ethan told her. "Prove you're human and tell your squadron to stand down."

"*You* prove it, Blackwood," she shot back. "And then you tell your people to stand down."

This was so frustrating.

Ethan wished there was a way he could trust her. He wished there was a way to find out if she was with the Ch'zar or not.

If Emma were here, she'd be able to tell. Emma would just reach out with her mind and either hear the song of the Ch'zar Collective inside Rebecca or not.

Ethan could do that . . . if he wasn't such a chicken. If he wasn't so scared that every time he heard the song, he'd go a little deeper into it, and one day go so far he wouldn't come back.

Not like there was a choice now.

So Ethan braced himself, reached out with his mind, and listened. He heard the pulses of anger and rage from the wasp and bee I.C.E.s, still wanting to tear at each other. But there was no choir of a million mental voices. No Ch'zar.

Rebecca was still Rebecca Mills.

"You're you," Ethan breathed.

She narrowed her eyes to slits. "How do you know that?"

"Look, I can just tell."

"Well, I can't," she said, and her face darkened. "Why the heck do you think we've been playing cat and mouse with Sterling Squadron all this time? We kept looking for a clue—some way to tell if you were you . . . or with them. Sure, we could see it was Sterling, but keeping the squadron flying is *exactly* the kind of trick the Ch'zar would pull if they were trying to lure any Resister survivors into the open. And there's just too much at stake to take any chances!"

Ethan heard the tension, the paranoia, and the desperation in her voice.

How could he prove he was still human? And quick? Before Felix and the others hurt one another? He had to make the first move.

He touched the communication link in his flight suit's collar, opening up the squadron channel.

"Back off," Ethan told Felix and Bobby. "It's Rebecca Mills and her bomber squadron in those bee I.C.E.s. So stop fighting! Zero in on my signal."

"Okay, Blackwood," Rebecca whispered, and slowly nodded. "We'll try it your way." She touched her collar. "You heard, people," she said. "Stand down. Come to me." She looked Ethan over once more. "But don't let your guard down."

"So . . . ," Ethan said. "Are we good?"

"Not by a long shot, Blackwood. I'm still expecting some Ch'zar trick." She shrugged. "I guess, though, it doesn't look like you hit puberty or anything in the last month . . . so maybe."

He tried to ignore the blushing that felt like it was burning off his face. "If I was Ch'zar," he told her, "I wouldn't need tricks. I'd just call in a thousand I.C.E.s from their factories." He waved his hand around. "They'd be here right now, digging you guys out of the earth. Instead, it's just me, Felix, and the rest of my squadron—Seed Bank survivors."

Rebecca gave a slight nod, sort of accepting this.

Three bees entered from one end of the tunnel. Felix's rhinoceros beetle and the Crusher praying mantis entered from the opposite side.

If they decided to mix it up, Ethan and Rebecca would be caught in the middle and squished.

"Ethan, are you okay?" Felix's voice boomed from his I.C.E.'s external speakers.

Bobby waved the mantis's long barbed forelimbs menacingly at Rebecca, who stuck her tongue out at the creature.

"We're cool," Ethan said, trying—and failing—to sound cool. He raised his hands in a gesture of peace.

Rebecca held up a hand, and her bees obediently halted.

Ethan envied the effortless way she commanded her people.

"So, Blackwood," she said, "assuming you are you, how did you and the rest of your crew make it here?"

Ethan took a deep breath and told her. He told her about how they'd flown as far and fast as they could to escape the explosion of the Seed Bank mountain, how they had found a hidden supply depot, and how they had discovered an old military base (he left out the details of his parents' letters, though).

"We spotted the massive Ch'zar military buildup here," Ethan continued, "by tapping into the aliens' satellite network. With the resources at our new base, we can see the entire planet."

Rebecca's eyebrows shot up at this. She chewed on her lower lip, thinking something over, then came to a decision. She met Ethan's gaze.

"You have a medical facility in this new, fancy base of yours?" she asked.

"Sure, it's huge. It has everything."

A hospital that was rusty and full of antiquated equipment they didn't know how to use, but Ethan left those details out.

"I guess I'm going out on a limb, Blackwood, but I don't have a choice."

Ethan shook his head, not understanding.

"We're not alone," she told him. "It wasn't just my squadron that made it out of the Seed Bank."

"There are other survivors?" Ethan asked, and stepped closer.

"There are more survivors," she said. "Not alive . . . but not exactly dead either."

° ° ° 16 ° ° °

PRECIOUS CARGO

STERLING SQUADRON AND REBECCA'S TEAM
landed on the flight deck at Titan Base. There was a
near riot as pilots dropped out of their insect cockpits
and ran across to each other, embracing, shaking hands,
and clapping each other on the back. It was like it was
everyone's birthday, New Year's Eve, and the start of
summer vacation all at once.

The Resisters on Ethan's side thought they were the
last free-willed humans left on the entire Earth. To see
Rebecca and her crew there among them—it seemed
too good to be true.

It was the first time in weeks that Ethan felt hope.

Rebecca's crew looked like they'd awakened from a terrible never-ending nightmare.

But Rebecca remained grim-faced. She crossed her arms over her chest and shouted out: "There'll be time for celebration later, group." She turned to Ethan. "We have to get our cargo to your medical facility ASAP. We've been racing the clock since this started. Which way is it?"

"You still haven't explained—" Ethan started.

Rebecca held up one hand. "I *will* explain. But later."

Ethan wanted to point out to Rebecca that this was *his* base, his command. But that was childish. Obviously she was worried. And it was clear that there was a crisis brewing. Issues like who was in charge weren't important right then.

Still, it bugged Ethan to have Rebecca calling the shots in front of his people.

She must have picked up on his feelings, because she paused, sighed, and said, "Please, Lieutenant. It's urgent."

"Yeah, sure," Ethan said. "Felix, give them a hand. Emma? Madison? Show Rebecca's people the way to the infirmary."

Madison and Emma saluted and immediately

moved toward the flight deck exit, leading Rebecca's people. Felix got Kristov and a half dozen other kids to help unload the luna moth carrier that Rebecca had ordered to rendezvous with their two squadrons en route back to Titan Base.

"If I might suggest, Lieutenant," Rebecca said, "you and I should lend a hand, too. I'll explain more as we walk."

Ethan followed her to the luna moth carrier. The I.C.E. had seen some action. Half its silvery scales were scorched. The inside cargo space, big enough to drive a truck through, was stacked to the top with cylinders nine feet long, three feet across, and made of brushed aluminum. There was a small window on each cylinder. A tiny computer display had been epoxied next to each window, and the display winked with graphs and symbols Ethan didn't recognize.

He peered though a window, but it was frosted over on the inside. He went to touch it, but instinctively jerked his hand away from the intense cold.

"Here." Rebecca grabbed two hydraulically powered hand trucks. Each of the wheeled units could lift and roll a half ton of cargo. She rolled one dolly at Ethan. She then checked the displays of several cylinders, found one she was looking for, and slid her hand truck under one end and dragged it out a bit.

Ethan wheeled his hand truck around and slipped the edge under the cylinder's other end. Together they rolled the cylinder off the moth and onto the flight deck. The hand truck registered a weight of only two hundred pounds. Whatever was inside was a lot lighter than Ethan expected.

But *what* exactly was he expecting?

They followed the line of other Resisters wheeling cylinders off the flight deck and into tunnel 414. The base's infirmary was near the flight deck. That made sense because that's where you'd expect injuries to come in.

Still, *close* on Titan Base meant a two-minute jog.

"This place is huge," Rebecca said, staring over her shoulder, back at the canyon-like walls of the flight bay.

"You have *no* idea," Ethan told her.

"Well, I guess before you tell me about this base," she said, "I owe you an explanation about us." She nodded at the cylinder. "And them."

Them? Ethan made a mental note. He bet it had something to do with her saying that there were more survivors . . . not alive . . . and not exactly dead either.

"After we bombed the lead Ch'zar command carrier at the Seed Bank," she said, still walking, "we got new orders from Colonel Winter."

With a chill, Ethan recalled how the colonel had ordered them to retreat, find a secret supply cache, and live to fight another day . . . while she then blew up the mountain containing the Seed Bank so the Ch'zar wouldn't get them.

Leaving the other Resisters behind had been one of the hardest things Ethan had ever done.

He blinked back tears. "Yeah, I remember."

"She ordered us *back* to base."

Ethan almost tripped, he was so surprised. He caught himself on the hand truck. "But the Seed Bank—"

"Yeah, blew up," Rebecca said. Her frown deepened so lines etched her forehead. "It was a superclose call that we didn't get blasted to atoms along with the rest of the mountain. We landed in an auxiliary hangar I didn't even know existed. Dr. Irving met us there and told us they had all sorts of contingency plans. He said, *'It was only a matter of time before the Ch'zar found us, my dear.'* Can you believe that?"

"Wait . . . you saw Dr. Irving *alive*? Was that before the place went sky-high?"

Rebecca stopped and took a deep breath. "It's complicated. Let me finish, and you'll understand everything when we get to the hospital."

Ethan nodded. It was going to kill him to *not* interrupt with a million questions, but he'd let Rebecca tell her story her own way.

They continued down the rusty corridor. Rebecca pulled the cylinder along a little faster now, as if to make up for the five seconds of lost time.

"So apparently the Seed Bank had miles of secret tunnels we kids never had a clue about," she said. "It was the old 'if-you-get-captured-by-the-Ch'zar-they'll-suck-out-everything-you-know-so-we're-not-telling-you-anything' excuse they were always pulling on us."

Ethan glanced ahead. "We're up there," he said, indicating the huge open double doors that led to the infirmary.

Rebecca picked up the pace now that they were close.

"They had supplies waiting for us," she told Ethan, "and new I.C.E.s prepped and good to go, so the Ch'zar wouldn't recognize my bumblebee bombers—which I'm still irked that I had to leave behind. My poor baby girls . . ."

They turned the corner and entered the west hospital wing. Madison and Emma were directing the kids to wheel the beds out of the way, so the cylinders could be lined up along the white tiled walls.

Rebecca tugged, spun their cargo about, and shoved it to the first spot in the infirmary.

"Those new, slimmer bee I.C.E.s, as you guys saw," she said with a slight smirk, "had a few tricks Dr. Irving had been prototyping: radar scramblers and advanced active camouflage like the new flight suits."

Rebecca pulled a crumpled page from her flight suit and smoothed it. On it were smeared, faded scribblings. "Okay, people!" she yelled. "I've got instructions from Dr. Irving. No one touch anything. This one is first."

At the mention of Dr. Irving, Madison's head snapped up. She started toward Rebecca.

Emma followed.

So did everyone else.

"Of course," Rebecca said in a whisper to Ethan, "those new systems on the I.C.E. bees came at a cost in weight and space. Dr. Irving stripped out all the weapons."

Ethan couldn't believe this. Maybe it was the fact that Dr. Irving and Colonel Winter hadn't picked him for this secret mission and had given it instead to Rebecca. Or maybe it was just that she had gotten to see Dr. Irving last.

Reading from the page, Rebecca tapped the computer display on the tube she and Ethan had wheeled in.

Madison got to them first, spun around, and motioned for the other kids to stand back. "Hold up," she said. "Give Sergeant Mills some breathing room to work."

Madison turned back to Rebecca and whispered, "What's this got to do with my grandfather? Did he write anything on that page for me?"

"Thirty seconds, Corporal," Rebecca muttered though gritted teeth, apparently not having the tolerance for Madison's questions that she'd had for Ethan's. Concentration made Rebecca's face a mask as she peered back and forth at the computer display and the page in her trembling hand, checking and rechecking what she was doing. "One way or the other," she whispered, "you're going to have all your answers."

Something didn't sound right with Rebecca. There was urgency in her normally ironclad, fearless tone.

Emma scooted closer to Ethan, her gaze intent on

a metal cylinder and the now furiously blinking display on the side. A puff of mist curled from the far end.

"I can feel something inside," Emma said so softly only he could hear. She reached out, and her hand hovered over the cylinder's surface.

Ethan didn't have to hold out his hand. He felt something now, too. A presence. Something that hadn't been in the cylinder a second ago. Something alive.

He took a step back, but Emma caught his hand and pulled him closer. A wry smile crept over her face.

The cylinder hissed. Ethan nearly jumped.

Everyone but he, Emma, and Rebecca took an involuntary step back.

A seam cracked the side of the cylinder. A lid hinged open.

Inside, it was filled with mist, which spilled out and across the floor, tendrils of vapor covering Ethan's boots and chilling his toes.

An object rose from the fog . . . impossible to see clearly.

Madison gasped and hurled herself at the thing.

Her motion dispersed the mist, revealing Dr. Irving, sitting up, puzzled, but nonetheless returning

Madison's hug. He rocked her back and forth as she wept with joy.

Dr. Irving then spotted Ethan and grinned. "Ah, Lieutenant Blackwood. Somehow I knew you and my granddaughter would be the first faces I saw when I woke up."

THE START OF WRONG

IT WAS A TEAR-FILLED REUNION. FELIX AND HIS mother, Colonel Winter, jettisoned proper military protocol and actually *hugged* in front of everyone. Madison couldn't stop sobbing—or smiling her crooked smile. Even Ethan had tears on his cheeks and a goofy grin.

The Sterling Academy recruits and Rebecca's team all high-fived.

Bobby and the Santa Blanca kids, though, kept apart from the celebration and stared warily at the new adults among them.

Colonel Winter looked exactly as Ethan had last seen her: dark hair streaked white down the center, blue uniform with a pistol strapped to one hip . . . and, as she detached from hugging her son, as cold and hard as an iceberg.

Everyone listened as she explained that they had always feared the Ch'zar might one day overrun the Seed Bank. There were contingency plans. They had cryogenic sleep tubes ready so that they could be placed inside in a state of suspended animation, then moved aboveground without risk of having their minds absorbed by the Ch'zar. Rebecca and her squadron were recalled at the last moment to sneak those cryo tubes past the aliens.

In addition, Dr. Irving had hidden supply depots of Resister technology, prototypes, and backups of their plans to fight the aliens in a dozen secret locations . . . so they could destroy the Seed Bank with little effect on the Resistance effort.

The destruction part of their plan was accomplished by simultaneously overloading the base's fusion reactors. They literally set off a dozen nuclear bombs to cover their tracks.

And of course, *none of this* had ever been revealed to active Resisters kids in case they were caught by the Ch'zar.

In all, fifty officers, eighty-eight technicians and scientists, and over thirty-eight kids too young for active duty had been evacuated. That was *almost* everyone from the Seed Bank.

There was a moment of silence for those who didn't make it . . . a few technicians who'd manned the base until the last moment . . . all the farm animals . . . and Jack Figgin's squadron, who'd died during the battle over the Seed Bank that day.

Naturally, the colonel and her senior staff immediately wanted a debriefing on Titan Base.

Ethan told her the truth about his parents' letters to Emma and him, and how they'd discovered the secret coordinates within them to this base. He did, though, leave out any possible explanations of *why* his parents had known about the base. He also left out the part about the picture he and his sister had found waiting for them here.

That part of the story felt like a private family matter.

As he did his best to explain everything, the colonel

and the other officers frowned and asked more probing questions.

Where were the original base inhabitants? Were any records left? Why didn't the Ch'zar know of the place? How did they so easily hack into the entire Ch'zar satellite network? Why were the robots on the lower decks out of control?

Ethan had no answers for them.

The colonel, her senior officers, and Dr. Irving then camped out in the base's Command Center, essentially taking the place over.

What else had he expected? They *were* the senior officers. They had more experience. They were supposed to be in charge, weren't they?

But they weren't including Ethan in their heated discussions and plans. He was there to answer their occasional questions, but otherwise he'd been told to keep his mouth shut.

Ethan felt a splinter of doubt stab inside him. Something was wrong with this entire scenario. . . .

If it hadn't been for him and his team no one would have ever found Titan Base. Rebecca would be low on supplies and still looking for a place to revive the adults—if the Ch'zar hadn't found her first.

The colonel and her staff kept flipping through the various views of the world, always coming back to the huge Ch'zar civil war raging on the Yucatán Peninsula.

Dr. Irving was off by himself, consulting data on a dozen smaller computer screens.

Ethan couldn't take it anymore. When the colonel and her officers were deep in some strategic debate, he edged over to the doctor.

Dr. Irving was so engrossed in his computer screens he didn't notice Ethan.

So Ethan cleared his throat.

The doctor turned, and the wrinkles of concentration etched onto his face smoothed. "Ah, Ethan, good, good. This base, while I have never heard of it, seems to be similar to installations under my command in the previous war. Same computers, languages, and systems. Still . . . I have questions about this satellite configuration."

"Doctor, I'm happy to answer any questions you have," Ethan said, his frustration creeping into his voice, "but can you answer a few of *mine*?"

The doctor cocked his head, startled. "Of course, young man. We've been waiting for this event all our lives. But I forget, you wouldn't even know about it. Personally, I thought it would take at least two more generations, another fifty years, before it started."

Ethan glanced at the doctor's computers to see if he could puzzle out what he meant.

The displays showed the same things he'd already seen: the miles and miles of factories in Central America and bugs fighting bugs.

There was one thing different. Ethan had seen it before, but it was new here. On one screen were the old Ch'zar population growth projections he and Madison had stumbled across a month ago. They showed the aliens' explosive expansion.

"They are preparing to swarm," Dr. Irving told Ethan. He took off his smudged reading glasses and polished them on the hem of his white lab coat.

"Like a hive of bees?"

"A close analogy, but missing a critical variation." Dr. Irving stood and went on in a lecturing tone of voice. "For *Apis mellifera*, or the common honeybee, when the hive population reaches a certain upper limit, and the food and weather conditions are favorable, the hive may shed a part of its population, which is given a new queen or queen egg. This portion then leaves the hive and relocates to establish a new colony. Thus, more bee-hives are in the world."

Ethan spotted the monitor directly behind Dr. Irving.

He held his breath. On it was a view of the moon, highly magnified. The indicators showed Ethan that the doctor had turned one of the Ch'zar's satellites around and pointed it into space.

It wasn't the moon, though, that both fascinated and horrified Ethan. Floating over the moon was the Ch'zar mothership.

Back when Ethan had first learned the truth about the aliens, Coach Norman had showed him a hologram of the alien spaceship. It was one-eighth the size of the moon, spiked and warty, with large areas of wide hexagons that made it look like an insect eye. But this ship was different than the image he'd seen that first time. That ship had been only partially constructed with open sections. This one looked almost done.

Worse . . . there were *two more* ships in orbit around the moon.

Those weren't quite the same as the first. One had hundreds of spikes. The other was perfectly smooth, not a single hexagonal plate. And these were only about two-thirds finished.

Seeing the ships made all the wrong Ethan had felt that afternoon seem like nothing. He swallowed the scream building inside him.

"The Ch'zar," he whispered. "Th-they're getting ready to swarm?"

"Indeed," Dr. Irving replied. "With one critical difference."

The doctor turned back to his monitors, removed his reading glasses, and used them to tap on one screen for emphasis. It showed an aerial view of the Yucatán factories burning, ant lion artillery blasting waves of locusts out of the air, red army ants sneaking in and overwhelming ant lions, and heavy moth bombers destroying *both* sides from a high-altitude run.

"This swarm apparently has a new rule. Only the strongest shall survive. While the Ch'zar population may be large enough to sustain three motherships, it appears they are having a 'disagreement' over the division of available resources to construct them.

"This may explain one long-standing mystery," Dr. Irving said as he gazed up and away, remembering something. "When the Ch'zar first arrived here, their original mothership had been heavily damaged. Some of us thought so much that it would never make another interstellar journey. We always surmised it was from a collision or other mishap. Now, it seems there may have been a civil war prior to their departure from their previous host planet. It may be their natural cycle."

Ethan stared at the battle, not knowing what he should be feeling. He was petrified by the destruction and violence—but also a little happy to see the Ch'zar killing each another—and there was something else: that feeling of *wrongness* that had been growing inside him since the adults woke up was solidifying into something he could almost make sense of.

"I hoped I would live to see this," Colonel Winter said. She stared at displays, nodding her approval.

Ethan jumped. She'd walked up without him having heard her boots clipping over the metal deck.

He saluted her. "Ma'am . . . why?"

"Because, Lieutenant, they are leaving," she said. "Fighting or not fighting, they've gotten what they wanted, and they are going." She took in a deep breath and then exhaled, looking pleased. "We'll finally be able to rebuild Earth."

That sounded like a good thing to him. So, why

then had the colonel's explanation only made him feel worse?

Dr. Irving set a hand on Ethan's shoulder. "You see, while we have trained you and the other Resisters to fight, it was never our ultimate goal to win. No. It would be foolish to fight to win against such a strong opponent. Instead, Ethan, our ultimate strategy has been to *outlast* the Ch'zar until they left."

Ethan turned to face the adults, shrugging off Dr. Irving's hand. "What if they don't go? What if only one of the motherships leaves and the other two stay . . . to finish their ships or just to dig in on Earth permanently?"

Colonel Winter's happiness faded. "That is a possibility, but again, Lieutenant, there is little we can do at this point."

"Or," Ethan whispered, now caught up in his thoughts and ignoring the colonel, "what if they do all leave?"

It finally dawned on him what he was feeling: fear, dread, and a building sense of responsibility that he had to do something about the Ch'zar once and for all.

"What if they leave and colonize *more* worlds?" Ethan asked. "They'll do what they did to Earth and humanity to another planet. To another people. If we don't stop them here and now, the Ch'zar will take over the whole galaxy!"

"Ethan . . . ," Dr. Irving said, and glanced at the colonel. "You may be right, but the bulk of Ch'zar battle forces are concentrated near the Yucatán factories and the Del Sol Equatorial Orbital Elevator. It is their manufacturing and supply line into low-Earth orbit and their motherships. Even if we had a hundred, a thousand I.C.E.s and pilots, they would still outnumber us a thousand to one."

Ethan shook his head. "There has to be a way."

"There is," Colonel Winter told him. "We wait. Let the aliens fight and kill each other. Let them leave. Then we will pick up the pieces."

Ethan kept shaking his head. "But we have to try something. There's more at stake than us and Earth."

All traces of understanding drained from the colonel's icy blue-gray eyes. "I commend your noble sentiments, Lieutenant, but there will be no more discussion on the matter. I want you to round up your people. We have to address the issue of these rogue robots on the lower levels."

A million possible plans swirled around in Ethan's head. "Ma'am, I—"

The colonel held up one hand to cut him off. "Assemble in the hangar bay in one hour. My senior staff will have a strategy."

Ethan couldn't believe the adults' plan was to do *nothing*—while the Ch'zar, for all practical purposes, were going to win!

Ethan hadn't fought so hard, for so long, to let the aliens win. And there was *no way* he was letting them leave Earth to do this somewhere else.

"I'm sorry," Ethan said, "I can't do that. I have to stop the Ch'zar. I *will* stop them."

"There is a time to fight," Colonel Winter told him, and tilted her chin up so she looked down on him, "and a time to wait. This is the latter."

Her glare seemed to bore into him, but Ethan stood tall and held his ground. "With respect, ma'am, I think it's time to fight—not be a coward."

That last bit slipped out before Ethan could stop himself. He knew it was a mistake to say it, but it was exactly how he felt. All the adults were being *chicken*.

"I see . . ." Colonel Winter narrowed her eyes to slits.

The temperature in the Command Center seemed to drop twenty degrees.

"Amanda," Dr. Irving whispered. He moved to set

a hand on her arm but then thought better of it and withdrew. "Perhaps we just need to explain the reasons better to Ethan."

"No," she said. "Words have never been ideal tools to communicate with Mr. Blackwood." She motioned for two guards and told them, "Escort the lieutenant to the brig. We have work to do and I have zero tolerance for insubordination."

The two adult guards grabbed Ethan by the biceps and marched him off.

Ethan struggled once, but the guards gripped harder. He looked back. Colonel Winter continued to glare at him. Dr. Irving shrugged, looking apologetic but resigned.

Ethan turned his back on the two adults he *thought* he had looked up to and admired.

They were so shortsighted and afraid.

Sure, Ethan was afraid, too, but he knew it was up to him to do the right thing.

At the moment, though, he wasn't sure just how he was going to get anything done from inside a prison cell.

∘ ∘ ∘ 18 ∘ ∘ ∘

IRONY

IT'D BEEN MONTHS SINCE ETHAN WAS IN HIS
English class at Santa Blanca's Northside Elementary
School, but he remembered one lesson in particular
that applied to this situation.

On irony.

Irony was when a reversal of what you'd expected
happened.

Like him getting locked into the same brig he'd ordered built from one of the base's hospital rooms.

The room had two beds, a tiny bathroom, tiled
floors and walls, and flickering overhead lights.

It was even more ironic that he was locked in the same prison cell as Paul Hicks—the person *he* had detained for insubordination, the same reason Colonel Winter had jailed Ethan.

Ethan had been frog-marched into the cell. The door slammed shut, and the welded bar slid in place behind him.

Paul Hicks had been too stunned to say anything. Instead, he laughed until he cried and then chuckled uncontrollably until he lay on his bed, holding his sides in pain.

He obviously hadn't seen the adult guards . . . or he'd have had questions.

"Shut up," Ethan told him.

"Yes, sir!" Paul snapped off a salute and started laughing again.

Ethan crossed his arms and sat in the corner on the other bed.

Felix and Kristov had welded the air ducts in this room tight. They'd checked the floor and ceiling, too, to make sure there'd be no way through them. There was no escaping this cell unless Ethan could trick the guards into letting him out.

He glanced through the tiny wire-reinforced window in the door.

There were two shadows on the opposite wall. The adult guards likely had orders directly from Colonel Winter to *not* listen to Ethan Blackwood, prisoner.

He sighed.

"So, Blackwood," Paul said, still chuckling, "tell me your sad, sad story."

"Why not?" Ethan said, and shrugged. "Maybe I'll see something I missed before . . . some way to convince her she's wrong."

Paul must have picked up on Ethan's dead-serious tone, because he stopped his inane chuckling. "Is anyone hurt?" he whispered. "Or dead?"

"No. But in some ways it's worse than one person getting killed."

Ethan ran through it all from the top—how they saw the Ch'zar fighting each other for resources on the Yucatán Peninsula. How the winner of that ongoing battle was then using the big beanstalk elevator at the equator to move materials into space. How there were three ships up there: possibly the original mothership that brought the aliens to Earth, being refit and repaired, and two entirely *new* spaceships.

The smile faded from Paul's scarred face as he connected the dots. "They're leaving?"

Ethan nodded. He had to give Paul credit—he'd pieced it together a lot faster than he had.

Ethan went on explaining how they'd found Rebecca and her squadron and then revived the adults who'd survived the destruction of the Seed Bank.

At this part of the story, disbelief, relief, and then concern and anger flashed across Paul's features. He kept his mouth shut, though, sat up, and leaned forward to hear more.

"I wanted to stop the Ch'zar," Ethan explained, "before the aliens could leave and enslave *another* world. Which is when the colonel and I had . . . a difference of opinion on the issue."

"But you were right," Paul whispered, cupping his chin with his palm, thinking.

Those were four words Ethan thought he'd never hear from Paul (at least not directed at him).

"Hey," Ethan said, "what *did* happen the other day? Why were you going through your preflight checklist on the mantis?"

Paul shrugged. "You wouldn't understand."

"Try me."

Paul looked at him a long time. "I just needed to . . . fly."

"Where?"

"Anywhere." Paul threw his hand up in frustration. "Across the hangar probably. I wasn't really thinking that far ahead. I just needed to get up into the air, to get away from this—you, all the others blindly following orders, everything. It all got to me."

"So, you weren't planning to run off?"

"Run?" Paul's eyebrows shot up. "Are you crazy? Where would I go? One I.C.E. wouldn't last long against the entire Ch'zar Collective." He dropped his gaze. "Besides," he whispered, "I'd die before I let them get me and betray you guys."

Ethan heard the sincerity in Paul's voice, and he believed him. On some level, Ethan could even sympathize with Paul. Sometimes, in the air was the only place Ethan could find peace.

"I'm sorry about hurting Kristov," Paul went on. "I panicked when he caught me going through my pre-flight on the mantis. I was scared when he caught up to me—he's so big, you know? The combat training kicked in and . . ." He sighed. "I wish I had the chance to say I'm sorry to him."

Movement in the corridor outside the room caught Ethan's eye. He jumped to his feet and peered through the tiny window. Two adults escorted a handcuffed girl down the hallway. He caught a glimpse just as they rounded the corner. Who had it been? Angel? Madison? And why would they be putting either one in jail?

Ethan wasn't sure. After all they'd been through, he thought they might be making progress in working out their differences.

"Blackwood!" Paul snapped his fingers. "Focus. So what's the plan?"

Ethan turned to face him but kept one eye on the door. "Plan?"

"To get out of here," Paul said, his face scrunched in irritation. "To stop the Ch'zar. To save the galaxy."

Ethan shook his head. "There is no plan."

Paul stood. "Don't be stupid. At least, more stupid than normal. You *always* have a plan."

More people appeared in the corridor outside the room. This time three guards with nightsticks prodded Kristov and Lee along. Kristov spotted Ethan looking out and gave him a thumbs-up as he passed. The two boys were locked into the room across from Ethan and Paul.

Ethan had that elevator-falling sensation in the pit of his stomach. What were his people all doing to get arrested? Getting in a massive fight? No. Kristov practically glowed with an aura of rebellion Ethan had seen before on the Sterling recruits . . . but his flight suit was unrumpled, and there wasn't a single scratch or bruise on skinny Lee (who surely would have shown some sign of a fistfight).

"Listen, Ethan," Paul said, and moved next to Ethan. "You're right, and the colonel is wrong. If we don't stop the Ch'zar they'll go off and enslave more people on more worlds. Beside, if some Ch'zar stay behind they're going to dig in and make Earth their permanent hive."

Ethan nodded. But what could they do?

Dr. Irving was also right. They were outnumbered a hundred thousand to one.

Oh . . . and there was one more irony. The Ch'zar were fighting each other. And instead of the humans taking advantage of that . . . they were fighting amongst themselves as well.

So stupid.

Worse—they had those robots on the lower levels to deal with before they found a way up here. There were so many of them. All armed with improvised weapons. In a pack he bet they'd be a match for an I.C.E.

Something about that notion stuck in Ethan's brain.

"Now you got it," Paul whispered. "I can see the old Blackwood brain ticking away. What is it?"

"The robots. On the lower levels of the base. They're like the ones we found in New Taos."

Those mechanical monsters had wanted to tear Ethan apart as well. And before that, the humans of that city had annihilated each other in World War IV.

Why was everyone *always* fighting?

But not every robot had tried to kill Ethan. There was that New Taos librarian robot (who'd been leaking enough radiation to kill Ethan if he'd stuck around too long anyway).

It had told him something . . . something that was superimportant . . . what?

He couldn't remember. He shook his head to jar his gray matter. No luck.

"Hey, isn't that Felix?!" Paul asked.

Ethan spun around.

Felix was indeed being marching down the corridor by two guards. Felix looked more pale than normal, and a sheen of sweat covered his face and neatly shaved head.

He looked up, met Ethan's worried gaze, and gave him a weak smile.

Ethan then knew exactly why his people were being tossed into jail.

Because of him.

They must have found out what the colonel had done. He imagined that, one by one, they disobeyed her orders as well. It was a full-blown mutiny.

Even Felix—the colonel's own son!

All for Ethan.

His heart twisted with guilt for getting them into hot water—but at the same time he was enormously proud of his team for sticking together.

Colonel Winter's angry face appeared in the door's window so suddenly that Ethan and Paul both jumped backward.

"Whoa!" they said.

The security bar slid aside, and Colonel Winter stood in the doorway, one hand resting on the handle of the ivory pistol always strapped to her side.

Two adult guards flanked her. Both men wore glares and frowns.

She pointed at Paul. "That one," she told the guards. "Remove him." The colonel told Ethan, "You and I will talk. Alone."

Paul looked from Ethan to the colonel and then the

guards. He raised one eyebrow, and his usual bravado seemed to return from whatever limitless well that he drew the stuff from.

"Heya, Colonel," Paul said, and tossed her a causal salute. "How's it going?" He then marched out with the two adults as if they were his personal honor guards.

"Sit," the colonel ordered Ethan, gesturing to one of the hospital beds.

Ethan remained standing.

"Please," she added icily. "We have a serious problem, beyond your individual insubordination, Lieutenant."

So it was *Lieutenant* again, was it? Ethan nodded. He moved to the bed and sat on the edge.

Colonel Winter sighed and sat on the other bed.

Ethan noticed two knuckle-shaped bruises on her chin.

"Your people are . . . ," she said, "well, to be commended on their loyalty to their commander. Especially the one called Angel." She absentmindedly rubbed her bruises. "Even Madison has seemed to take leave of her senses on this matter."

"And Felix?" Ethan whispered.

The colonel's face tuned to stone.

"Each and every pilot, as well as the new Santa

Blanca refugees, refused to take orders from anyone but their squadron commander—after they somehow learned of your predicament. I had no choice but to throw them all in the brig, to cool off . . . before I press official charges."

When she said *cool off*, the colonel took in a deep breath and blasted out the exhale, as if admitting that *she* was the one who needed to cool off.

Ethan pondered it all, and after a moment of silence, said, "Shouldn't we be fighting the real enemy instead of fighting amongst ourselves?"

The colonel blinked and stared at Ethan, then stared through Ethan for a time—then refocused on him. "That is exactly what I came to speak with you about. You need to reason with them, Ethan. We are in this together. They must stand down."

"Stand down . . . ?" Ethan whispered.

Those two words stuck in his head. They felt like a key that had been inserted into his brain and that was slowly turning, unlocking a treasure chest of memories.

Where had he heard *stand down* before? It was so close. Something connected with . . .

"The robots," he said.

The colonel looked confused.

But Ethan had it now. The other pieces of how it *had* to work all clicked into place.

He had to stand he was so excited.

"I know how to win," he told the colonel. He smacked a fist into his palm. "Win so big the Ch'zar will *never* recover."

She eyed Ethan like he'd lost his mind. "I don't think you appreciate the position you and your people are in."

Ethan forced himself to calm down. He sat.

She was right. He had to win one battle at a time. First he had to forge a truce between the free-willed human adults and the kids.

"I understand our position, ma'am. I will talk to my people as you suggest. I need to actually talk to *everyone*, though." Ethan's words then came in a great rush: "I need to explain my plan to stop the Ch'zar once and for all. . . . I want you to hear me out—really hear me out. All of your staff, too—and especially Dr. Irving, he's the key to the first part—and after you hear . . ."

He took in a gulp of air, and slowed. "After I've explained it all, if you think it's crazy or not worth the risk, then I'll do as you've ordered. I'll tell the squadron that we're going to stand down and let the Ch'zar leave."

She still looked at him, unblinking.

Ethan couldn't tell what she was thinking. That'd he'd snapped? That she better order a quick, improvised firing squad to assemble on the flight deck?

He detected a tiny flicker in her gray-blue eyes. Not warmth, but maybe . . . some microscopic acknowledgment that he wasn't a complete idiot.

"We will hear you out then, Mr. Blackwood," she said. "When you're a bit older, I think I'm going to enjoy playing poker with you."

∘ ∘ ∘ 19 ∘ ∘ ∘

CRAZIEST AND BEST PLAN EVER

EVERYONE GATHERED ON THE CENTRAL STAGE of Titan Base's Command and Control Center.

Ethan's entire squadron was there. There were the original Resisters: Felix, Madison, and even Paul. There were the Sterling recruits: Lee, Oliver, Kristov, Angel, and of course, his sister, Emma. There were also Bobby, Sara, Leo, and the other kids recused from Santa Blanca.

They had gravitated to one side of the circular platform, with hostile glares, arms crossed.

Facing them was Colonel Winter, her stare unblinking, cold steel; Dr. Irving, looking wise and in control and a little apologetic; along with the senior staff, adult technicians, and the younger kids brought from the Seed Bank who had no clue what was going on.

Between these two groups, in neutral territory, stood Rebecca and her bomber squadron. She kept glancing back and forth between the groups, with what looked like a hopeful smile.

Ethan had found out from Felix that Rebecca hadn't disobeyed orders like everyone in Sterling had . . . but she had expressed her disappointment with them to Colonel Winter.

This was Ethan's chance to prove to the adults that he wasn't crazy—or at least, that his plan wasn't—and that they could just maybe win the war with the Ch'zar if they listened to him.

He was in the middle of the Command Center stage. The spotlights overhead that usually focused on various computer stations were now all trained on him.

It was hot. He tried not to sweat in his flight suit in front of everyone, but it was pointless. Even if he'd stood in the Antarctic, Ethan would have been sweating.

Everything was riding on this. On him.

"Go ahead, Lieutenant," Colonel Winter said, loud enough for all to hear. "We'd like to see this plan you have."

There was no sarcasm, not a hint of disapproval in her voice, but Ethan nonetheless heard something . . . dangerous.

"The plan," Ethan said. He stopped. His mouth was suddenly as dry as beef jerky. He swallowed and tried again. "The plan has a lot of parts," he said, "so I'll ask everyone to be patient until I can go over the entire thing."

The colonel nodded.

Okay. She was going to let him do this. He'd half expected her to change her mind and turn this into a court-martial.

Ethan strode to a computer station and tapped in a command. The live images of the three Ch'zar space-ships near the moon appeared on the huge wall. The ships looked like magnified images of spiky, weird pollen grains he'd seen in his fifth-grade science books. Only these pollen grains were four hundred miles across.

There were many gasps from the crowd. Not everyone there, especially the little kids, had seen the alien ships before.

"There are three Ch'zar ships being built," Ethan explained. "The big, more finished one was constructed from what we think was left of the original ship that came to Earth fifty years ago. As Dr. Irving explained to me, this shipbuilding is a swarming behavior of the alien insect collective. But as they're running out of resources on Earth, it looks like the three ships are now fighting over the last materials they'll need to make the long trip to a new solar system. The two weaker and smaller sides are against the larger, stronger one . . . which still looks like it's going to win."

On-screen, tiny flashes and fireballs appeared in the space between the massive vessels.

Ethan adjusted the controls and pulled back from the extreme long view, until Earth appeared as a slice of blue and white whirls at the edge of the screen.

"We're going to change the balance of power between these sides," he said.

A line came into view, running from the clouds of Earth up until it vanished into the black. Ethan zoomed in. As he got closer, the thickness of the line, which at first appeared to be like a fine thread, showed itself to actually be a hundred feet across with sealed elevator pods flashing up and down at high speed. On every mile-long girder clung a huge black dung beetle, huddled close to the structure, missile pods bristling outward.

"This is the Del Sol Equatorial Orbital Elevator," he said, "sometimes called the beanstalk. It's the enemy's major lifting mechanism to get things into space. Dr. Irving tells me this one structure moves eighty percent of Earth's stolen resources into space for the Ch'zar. Currently it's controlled by the guys with the one big ship."

Dr. Irving looked over his glasses at the image. "Quite true on all counts," he said.

"We're going to blow that space elevator up," Ethan confidently told everyone. "That'll give the two weaker sides a chance to regroup to fight the bigger ship before it can be finished. The Ch'zar may cause more damage to themselves than we ever could."

There were shouts and cheers from Sterling Squadron, looks of utter disbelief from the adult side, and Rebecca looked too stunned to react . . . until she slowly raised a hand to ask a question.

Ethan held up both arms for quiet and pointed at Rebecca.

"Lieutenant," she said, "I don't mean this to sound like I'm not behind you. . . ." She took a long look around at everyone and scratched the side of her closely shorn hair. "But there are two things that'll stop us. The Resistance has looked at that target before. Higher on the beanstalk there are hundreds of Vampire-class tick I.C.E. single-shot missile launchers. It's the only place the Ch'zar have medium-range missiles deployed. That makes the only approach near ground level. And even at maximum speed, my bombers would never make it through the surrounding industrial sector. There's too much ant lion artillery."

Sterling Squadron's cheers died to silence at this. They all respected Rebecca.

"I know," Ethan replied. "I'll show you in a moment how we're going to get past their defenses. But what's the other thing you think could stop us? You said there were two?"

"Well . . ." Rebecca's gaze dropped, and she chewed her scarred lip. "We don't have any bombs left, sir. In the last battle at the Seed Bank we used up the heavy ones. And without majorly big bombs you're not going to be able to take out the beanstalk. It's just too well built."

The rest of her bomber squadron, experts in blowing stuff up, nodded in total agreement.

Ethan allowed himself a tiny smile and then quickly wiped it off his face.

"That's not a problem," Ethan told her, and tapped a button. "This is video from our last recon mission."

A new, shaky image projected onto the Command Center wall. It showed the Yucatán factories and warehouses from three thousand feet.

A tiny shadow fell over one warehouse. A split second later, a pulse of light flashed across the scene and lanced the object casting the shadow as it came into view.

The blur of an object erupted into a huge sheet of fire that boiled over the buildings, then exploded, flattening three of the structures into smoldering shrapnel.

There was a collective intake of breath at the impressive carnage.

"That was only a partly filled extra fuel tank dropped on our recon mission," Ethan said. "Angel decided, uh . . . as an experiment, to laser-detonate the thing, and that's what happened. I think we'd get an even better explosion with a full tank."

"Air-fuel bombs," Dr. Irving stated with a deep nod. "Such devices were used in the last human war. They were usually considered too dangerous for conventional operations. They were, however, extraordinarily powerful. I think the yield of these fuel-tank bombs could be significantly boosted with an internal explosive to disperse the fuel over a larger area."

Colonel Winter raised her eyebrows at Dr. Irving.

"It's true," he told her. "Three or four should be sufficient, if properly placed, to demolish the orbital elevator."

Rebecca's pilots whispered excitedly to one another.

"Getting to the beanstalk elevator is the next part of the plan," Ethan told everyone. "Like Rebecca said: there's too much ant lion artillery to make a bombing run at the tower . . . unless we counter with an army of our own."

The crowd murmured, but all fell quiet as Ethan tapped in a new command on his computer.

On the wall screen, security video appeared, grainy black and white and distorted along the edges. Ethan, Emma, Angel, and Bobby appeared for a second in the frame—running for their lives. A pack of wheeled maintenance robots raced after them.

The camera changed and showed those robots pounding and ripping through a steel wall near a security door to get at Ethan and his friends.

"Four or five of these robots, armed with weapons such as rivet guns or plasma welders, would be a match for a Ch'zar I.C.E.," Ethan stated. "With enough of them, we'd have a great diversionary force."

He tapped once more on the computer keyboard.

"Excuse me," the colonel said.

She looked a bit too smug for Ethan's liking. "Yes, ma'am?"

"Aren't these the same robots that tried to *kill* your team? What makes you think they will target the Ch'zar?"

Many on Sterling Squadron, especially Bobby and Emma, looked especially concerned at this. Who could blame them? They'd almost gotten pulped by the rolling death machines.

"Because, Colonel," Ethan replied, "I believe we have a way to control the robots."

He turned to Dr. Irving, and the old scientist smiled at him. This was one place Ethan's plan could fall apart. He hadn't been able to consult with Dr. Irving ahead of time. Ethan just hoped he'd guessed right.

"Dr. Irving, you once told me that you were a general in the last great human war. Is that correct?"

Surprised whispers erupted from everyone in the Command Center, and all eyes turned to the doctor. Apparently this had been a secret. But it had to come out, if Ethan was going to make his plan work.

Dr. Irving's bent frame straightened. His gentle smile faded, and he looked more confident (and scary) than Ethan had ever seen the man.

"Indeed, Lieutenant," he said. "But I was not *a* general in the last great war. I was *the* general."

"And you said this base, even though you never knew about it, used the same systems as the side you were on in that war? So it stands to reason it was under the same military command."

Dr. Irving nodded as he mulled this over this. "Possibly . . ."

Ethan made a slow turn as he spoke so everyone could see his face. "When Sterling Squadron was in New Taos a few months ago, we ran into sentry robots similar to the maintenance bots here . . . except they were armed with plasma cannons." He shuddered at the memory of nearly getting parboiled by those machines.

"There was one robot there that was different, though," Ethan told them. "The librarian. When I asked it if there was a way to stop the sentry robots from killing us, it told me it could cancel the defense protocol . . . if I had a level-three authorization code."

Dr. Irving's head jerked up, and a sly grin spread over his features as he understood where Ethan was going with this.

"Is there any chance," Ethan asked him, "that you have a level-three security authorization code that might work here?"

Colonel Winter set a hand on Dr. Irving's arm to get his attention, but he ignored her.

"Level three?" Dr. Irving said. "No . . . but I do have a level-*five* authorization code."

"Great," Ethan breathed as relief flooded through his body. He wanted to sit down, but there was more.

"There's one more piece of the plan that I have to show everyone. Emma?"

He motioned for his sister to come forward. She did, giving a little wave to everyone, then sat at the computer by Ethan and started opening blueprint files of the base.

"The robots have severed the command circuits coming from this room to the lower levels," Ethan said, "but my sister found an auxiliary robot control room."

Emma projected a schematic of Titan Base on the wall—sprawling tunnels, reactors, and machine bays that went on for miles and miles, over fifty levels deep. The view zoomed into level thirty-seven.

"The command circuits appear to be intact," Ethan said, "but we're going to have to get down there and manually input the security authorization code."

He let that sink in a moment. Everyone looked like they got it, but there were some shaking heads and narrowed glances.

"Remember why we're doing this, though," he said. "If we blow up the beanstalk elevator, that'll give the two weaker Ch'zar sides a chance to fight the larger, winning side in space. It'll do more damage to the aliens than anything the human Resistance could do to them in a *hundred* years. Maybe save not only us, but the next race the Ch'zar tries to enslave."

Ethan was out of breath.

Everyone in the Command Center was utterly silent. All eyes turned to Colonel Winter.

"The Ch'zar fighting each other, yes," she whispered, and her gaze defocused. "I see the strategic brilliance of that." She tapped her lower lip, thinking. "A bomb run with air-fuel devices—risky, but not without precedence in the scope of previous Sterling Squadron missions . . ."

Her focus returned and her gaze fixed on Ethan. "But the robot part of your plan, Lieutenant. There are so many unknowns. Can we get to the auxiliary robot controls? Can they be reprogramed? How many of these units are there? Will they successfully engage with the Ch'zar so your people can advance to the orbital elevator?"

"I know . . . ," Ethan admitted.

He started to feel the room spin. He leaned against the computer station and took a deep breath.

Emma reached out to steady him, but he gave her a quick shake of his head. He couldn't look weak in front of the others, not now.

The colonel could shut down Ethan's plan.

He'd promised her that he would abide by her decision.

Would the others in his squadron go along? Was this the start of the riskiest Resister operation ever? Or the flashpoint of a full-blown mutiny, kids versus the adults? Or would they all just sit here, safe, but let the Ch'zar win?

The colonel shifted her focus to the schematic of

the base projected on the wall. She lifted a finger and traced one particular path.

"I think I can help with this last part of our plan," Colonel Winter said, and the slightest smile flickered over her pale lips. "After all, I have *some* expertise in operational strategy as well."

Our plan? Did Ethan hear right?

"Assemble your strike team, Lieutenant," she said, and stood. "I suggest three to five. Excellent rope skills are required. Having passed the basic firefighting course will also be mandatory."

Ethan blinked. "So . . . we're going to do it?"

The colonel looked at Ethan for a long time. She then saluted him. "Absolutely. Why wouldn't we?"

Ethan suppressed a wild grin. He turned to glance at his squadron, then turned back to the colonel and snapped off a crisp salute. Behind him he heard the entire squadron repeat the gesture of respect.

They were going to do this. They were going to fight.

Why then, all of a sudden, did Ethan feel like his crazy plan just might have been an *impossible* plan?

... 20 ...

FIRE IN THE HOLE

ETHAN LEANED OVER AND PEERED DOWN THE maintenance shaft. He gulped. It was a straight fall thirty-four levels through darkness. Certain death if their rope or rappelling gear failed.

Then there were the robots. He heard a distant mechanical echo. Deep in the darkness, there was a spark.

They were down there. Waiting . . . watching . . . planning, he bet, for some stupid kid to come wandering down there.

Like him.

Emma handed Ethan a silvered helmet.

This was the other complication to their descent: thermal heat suits used to fight fires on the flight deck. You could stand in burning jet fuel for three minutes in one of these things. They were sealed head to toe with their own internal air supply. Really, they were more like space suits.

"Ready?" Ethan asked.

Emma and Oliver wore the same silvery suits. They both nodded.

"Weapons check," Emma said.

Ethan made sure he had his gear. They all had hand-held plasma welding torches, a rivet gun, and a canister contraption engineered by Dr. Irving. He had called it an electromagnetic grenade and guaranteed it would scramble the electronic brains of any robot they detonated it near. He had warned them *not* to use it near the auxiliary robot control room, or they'd fry the computers there and the entire operation would be wasted.

Ethan pulled his helmet on snug. His heart raced. There was no going back now.

"Felix," he said over his helmet's radio. "You and Big Blue ready?"

"As ready as we'll ever be," Felix replied.

His rhinoceros beetle lumbered down the B-4

corridor of level three. The huge I.C.E. didn't fit in here. It had, however, *made* itself fit by pushing and shoving on the walls, ceiling, and floor deck like the steel was tinfoil. Pipes and electrical conduits cracked and burst as the bug pushed up to the maintenance shaft. It stuck its horned head into the open space, cratering the wall as it did so.

"You guys better back up," Felix said. "There's ventilation up and down this shaft, but some plasma is bound to splash out our way."

"Roger that," Ethan said. The three silver-clad Resisters jogged back and around a corner.

He had thought *his* plan was crazy—but the colonel's plan to get them down to level thirty-seven was a doozy!

The problem was this: Security cameras showed that all the elevators, elevator shafts, and stairs to the lower levels were guarded by 'bot patrols. No one was getting down there without a *major* battle.

There was this one maintenance shaft, though, that had no visible robot guardian. It went straight to level thirty-seven. The one catch? It was only two and a half feet wide. The colonel had also told him there was likely to be at least one small robot guard watching the access point.

That's where Ethan and his small strike team came in. That's where Felix and his beetle I.C.E. came in as well.

First, the I.C.E. would muscle its way in there and then let loose a blast of plasma from its class-C particle cannon. That would eliminate any robotic threat in or near the shaft. It would also heat the metal to almost the melting point!

Not as big as the adult Resisters, Ethan and his team would fit in the space and be able to rappel down the red-hot pipe.

From the exit point on level thirty-seven, it was then a short three-hundred-foot stroll to the robot control room.

Simple.

. . . And in a million ways, deadly.

The rhinoceros beetle's horns flared white-hot. The air between them sparked and glowed like the aurora borealis. A wash of superheated plasma shot down the shaft, and then almost immediately backwashed— boiling down the rumpled corridor toward Ethan.

He ducked around the corner just before he got roasted (firefighting suit or not!).

The beetle backed away from the glowing semi-molten hole crushed in around the maintenance shaft. "You guys are up," Felix said.

Ethan, Emma, and Oliver trotted to the hole. Ethan clipped his steel line to a sturdy I beam and tossed the long coil down the shaft. He threaded his rappelling rack to the line and clamped tight, then eased his body out over the hole.

Air rushed up, a blast of furnace heat around him. If he hadn't had the silver suit on, he'd have been toast.

The edges of the maintenance shaft flickered a faint red all the way down. The air wavered with heat like a desert mirage.

Was he *really* going to do this?

He had to. It was only a matter of time before the robots figured out what was going on. The clock was ticking.

"Good lu—" Felix started to say.

But Ethan had already pushed off and zipped down the line.

He bounced off the side. Even in the silver heat-resistant suit the wall was still blazing hot. Ethan instinctively straightened his body, wrapping his legs around the line, and like an arrow, plummeted down faster.

His pulse thundered in his chest and ears, and he felt squeezed on every side. Sweat fogged up his faceplate. This must be how a steamed dumpling felt.

He spotted a robot that had been inside the shaft— just a flash and a blur, but enough of a glimpse to see it was cat-sized and half melted and plastered to the side of the tube, its limbs struggling to pull itself free.

Ethan's line counter beeped. He was getting close to level thirty-seven.

He squeezed the rappelling rack's brake and sparks showered up around him . . . but he slowed . . . and then stopped, dangling before an access hatch.

Ethan turned the wheel on the small round door and climbed out of the shaft and into a pitch-black corridor.

At least it was cooler. He waited for the others, panting, sweat dripping into his ears and eyes. He didn't need his helmet anymore, so he pulled it off, and sucked in cold air.

What a relief!

Ethan didn't need the helmet anymore because

there was *no* way he was going to climb up that maintenance shaft. He'd find a different route back.

There was a *twang* on the steel line, a *whoosh* of hot air from the open hatch, and then sparks.

Emma appeared, bobbling on the line. Ethan helped her out into the tunnel.

Oliver came down a split second later. He climbed out fast by himself, ripping off his helmet. His glasses were bent and completely fogged. He gasped in huge gulps of air.

Ethan set a hand on his shoulder. "It's okay," he told him. "We made it."

Emma took off her helmet as well. She uncoiled her braid from around her neck and inhaled deeply. She then got out a pen flashlight and played its light over the tunnel.

LEVEL XXXVII had been stenciled on the rusted steel wall.

"We're in the right place," Ethan said.

Oliver spun around, then turned left. "I memorized the blueprints. The robot control room is this way."

° ° ° 21 ° ° °

QUIET, NOT QUITE

THEY ALL GOT OUT ONE OF THEIR WEAPONS.
Emma picked up her handheld welder. Ethan hefted
his rivet gun. Oliver had one of the electromagnetic
grenade canisters.

"There's a junction a hundred feet ahead," Emma
said. "We turn right, go two hundred more feet, and
then the door we want is on the right." She flashed Oliver a look. "You're not the only one who memorized
the blueprints of this place."

"Sort out who's the bigger brainiac later, please,"
Ethan whispered. "Let's move fast *and* quietly."

Oliver and Emma nodded and followed him.

So far, so good. No robots. Funny . . . but Ethan hadn't even heard the machine clanging they'd heard before down here. Maybe it was just a lucky break.

He and Emma both suddenly stopped.

Ethan had a weird ringing in his skull. It was the same thing he'd felt in New Taos. Emma put two fingers on her forehead as if she was in pain.

He shook off the odd sensation and motioned Emma and Oliver to keep moving.

That ringing had to be some computer communication he and his sister were picking up. There'd been a complex network of mechanical minds in New Taos. He bet there was something like that going on down here. Ethan wouldn't underestimate the intelligence of these maintenance 'bots.

They got to the intersection, and Ethan let Emma and Oliver fall against one wall, then signaled a halt with his raised fist.

He carefully peered around the corner.

And froze.

Peering back at him with their three-camera-lens eyes were four robots, each the ten-foot-tall, quarter-ton variety. One held a parabolic antenna with a wire from it plugged into its head. The antenna had been hammered together from squished tin cans.

They weren't moving, though. Not a single gear whirled. Not one diode flashed.

Ethan's heart started beating again. Maybe they were in some sort of sleep mode?

He'd have to find another way around.

He started to pull back . . . when his elbow popped.

The robot with the antenna instantly pointed the device in Ethan's direction. In its other hand, it held an air horn—which it used. A blaring foghorn note filled the air!

The other robots woke up and surged forward, pulling out *their own* weapons: a whirling chain saw, a length of electrified chain, and a hundred-pound sledgehammer!

Plans of action raced through Ethan's brain: split up, run, distract the 'bots so Emma and Oliver could get away, try to reason with the mechanical men, fight!

Except one.

"The grenade!" Ethan cried to Oliver.

Oliver was ready. The canister whistled over Ethan's head. It hit the robot with the chain saw, and the grenade clattered to the deck.

There was a flash of light and a rapid strobe from Dr. Irving's device.

Sparks washed over the robots and along the steel walls, ceiling, and deck. The mechanical creatures seized and toppled over onto each other in a heap.

The ringing in Ethan's skull spiked and vanished.

"That got 'em," Emma said, and leaped over the inert robots. "Come on, hurry. They're all going to know where we are now."

Ethan ran after her. She was right.

He dropped his rivet gun and pulled out his grenade.

As they sprinted, Emma's and Oliver's flashlights made crazy dancing patterns on the walls.

One pattern stayed. A long line of shadows ahead that got closer and closer.

Four more robots entered the tunnel a hundred feet ahead of them.

Emma skidded to a halt at the door on her right. "This is it!"

Ethan *had* to use his grenade—or they'd be flattened. But how close was *too* close to the robot control room? If he overloaded the computers inside, this mission was over.

He hucked the grenade as far as he could. Staying alive for the next five minutes was the priority.

The grenade bounced and rolled into the oncoming blitz of robots.

A brilliant flash painted the sharp, shadowy outlines of the enemy pack onto the walls.

The 'bots screeched to a grinding halt. Dead.

Emma and Oliver got the door open.

"Oliver, stay here," Ethan said. "Keep your eyes and ears peeled."

Oliver's eyes widened, half panicked now. He obeyed, though, and stayed behind as Ethan and Emma rushed into the room.

The space was tiny, no bigger than a glorified closet. Covering the walls were pinned-up schematics of various types of maintenance robots. There were the big mono-wheeled ones, smaller ones with four wheels, and even a plum-sized one with suckers for hands and feet.

On the far side of the closet were a desk, a computer terminal, and a chair.

Emma and Ethan raced for the computer.

Ethan got there first, sat, and hit the ON switch.

It took four heartbeats for the screen to warm up and the cursor to appear. The keyboard was covered with dust and mummified mouse droppings.

"I hear grinding," Oliver hissed in a low whisper. "Coming down the tunnel!"

On the computer screen the following flashed:

```
ACCESS DENIED
ULTRAHIGH SECURITY PROTOCOLS
IN EFFECT
ENTER OVERRIDE CODE
>>
```

"Hurry," Emma told him. She got out her grenade— the *last* grenade.

"More incoming," Oliver said, his voice a mere squeak of fear. "I hear them coming from *both* sides. . . ."

Ethan pounded on the keyboard, typing as fast as he could. Dr. Irving's code was ALLQUIETONTHE-WESTERNFRONT. He'd told Ethan his level-five authorization code was the title of a very old book, a very good one, and one that Ethan should read someday.

Ethan would very much like that—*if* he lived that long.

The computer screen blanked and then:

```
ACCESS DENIED
ULTRAHIGH SECURITY PROTOCOLS
IN EFFECT
ENTER OVERRIDE CODE
>>
```

Emma bent closer. "I bet you mistyped *quite* instead of Q-U-I-E-T. You were always doing that on your school reports."

"I can *see* them," Oliver said, all emotion drained from his voice he was so scared. "There are 3000 many, Ethan."

Emma turned and cocked her arm to huck her grenade.

Ethan focused. How could a typo kill you?!

He tried again . . . as carefully as he could . . . as fast as he *dared*.

ALLQUIETONTHEWESTERNFRONT

He held his breath.

```
CODE ACCEPTED
ULTRAHIGH SECURITY PROTOCOLS
CANCELED
```

Robots rolled to a stop outside the room, crowding each other and peering in. One dropped its chain saw and set a light hand on Oliver's head as if patting a little kid.

Oliver's knees wobbled, but he remained standing.

"Excuse us, sirs," a robot asked. "Are you in need of any assistance?"

Ethan almost fell out of his chair. "I think," he said to the robots, "a little bit, yes, if you don't mind."

22

BENCHED

IT FELT LIKE OLD TIMES WHEN ETHAN HAD STUD-
ied all the plays before a school soccer game.

This game, though, was much, much bigger
with thousands of players on either side. And winning wasn't about breaking records or taking home
a championship trophy. It was about the continued
existence of the human race, and maybe the freedom
of a dozen other intelligent species on other distant
worlds.

He stood in the flight bay by a cart used to service
their I.C.E.s. On the top of the cart was a flattened map

of the Yucatán Peninsula. The map had lines, circles, and arrows drawn over it.

This was Ethan and the colonel's joint plan of attack.

It showed how their new robotic forces would move over the terrain and strike the Ch'zar forces—with the sole purpose of distracting them, so Ethan's team would make it to the beanstalk elevator and blow the thing up (or in this case, *down*).

Simple. Just like making a soccer goal across an incredibly well-defended field.

More reassuring than any plan, though, were his sister and friends.

Standing around the cart and going over the last details with him were Madison, Emma, and Felix. They were the three people he trusted most in the world.

He couldn't do this without them.

"One more load to go," Emma said, and nodded across the flight deck.

"Don't they all freak you out?" Madison whispered to Ethan.

Ethan looked as the last of the maintenance robots had lined themselves in a neat rectangle, ten by one hundred units strong. Three thousand camera eyes focused and refocused and stared straight back at Ethan.

The robots were totally motionless, but not inert. They were ready for action, listening intently for his next order.

"It's the creepy cameras they have for eyes," Ethan told Madison. "I get the feeling these robots were never meant to interact much with the base's people. So no one cared how they looked."

Felix folded his big arms over his chest. "I still don't trust them," he said. "They try to kill us one minute, then they're ready to lay down their lives for us the next."

"It's binary, zeroes and ones, for them," Ethan said.

He reached out with his mind, imagined he could feel the computer code—little ons and offs, white and black dots all flitting across their microprocessor brains.

"They think in absolute terms: friend or foe," Ethan continued. "We had the *friend* code. So, we're friends."

"More than that," Emma added with supreme confidence. "We're their masters."

Felix was right, though. It was strange to see the robots so ultraobedient. What if something went wrong in their computer minds? Electronic glitches happened all the time. Look what happened to the robots in New Taos, trying to repair a city for humans that were long dead.

There had been *so* many maintenance robots in the lower levels. Ethan guessed that Titan Base, with miles and miles of passages and hundreds of rooms, had needed a literal army to keep it in running order.

At last count they had over seven thousand robots of various sizes and abilities now ready to fight for the Resistance.

It'd taken a day to round them up on the flight deck and start shipping them out to the staging area in Mexico.

Ethan tapped a red circle on the map. "We sure no Ch'zar are onto us?"

Madison touched her ear and listened to her radio link. "Latest report just coming from the staging area, sir. One of Rebecca's people en route back to base. All robots on perimeter patrol detect no inbound Ch'zar. Half a dozen of Becka's bees are in the tree canopy, camouflaged, and have eyes in the sky." Madison refocused her green-eyed gaze on Ethan. "And we're still getting images from the Ch'zar satellites overhead. I think we're good."

"Good," Ethan said, careful to not let his anxiety be heard by the others. He had to lead them into this battle with confidence, even if he didn't feel it.

"On-ground weapons status?" he asked Felix.

Felix consulted a data pad.

"Latest report shows all portable fusion reactors set up in the staging area," he said. "We'll have every weapon charged two hours before dawn."

"Just in time," Ethan said. "Good work."

The fusion generator power was for the robots and their weapons.

At first, Ethan thought the odds were stacked against them. The robots' weapons—chain saws and sledgehammers—would have been pitiful against Ch'zar I.C.E. armor. Dr. Irving, though, had rigged flamethrowers, rail-gun rifles, mortar launchers, sonic blasters, and a half dozen other nasty (and very cool) instruments of destruction.

On top of that, the robots had offered to help; otherwise it could have taken months to get the weapons made. A thousand robots had scavenged the base for parts, while another two thousand had formed a line to put all the weapons together.

It was like a self-assembling army.

That left one last thing to triple-check.

"The air-fuel bombs," Ethan asked Emma. "What's their status?"

"Dr. Irving said he was going over the wiring one last time," Emma said, her voice deadly serious.

Dr. Irving had insisted that only he be allowed to assemble the bombs. One mishap, one of those things detonating inside Titan Base . . . and it'd put an end to this operation.

It'd most likely put an end to the Resistance.

On the far side of the flight bay the last of their I.C.E.s that hadn't been dispatched were parked: Ethan's gold-and-black wasp, Felix's midnight-blue beetle, Emma's ladybug (close to Felix's I.C.E.), and Madison's gleaming emerald dragonfly.

That's where Dr. Irving had set up his work area. Inside a protective ring of I.C.E.s were empty spare fuel tanks, fuel trucks, and a dozen carts with tools, electronics, and moldable plastic explosives.

Dr. Irving had constructed five of what he called thermobaric devices. He also called them the biggest bombs this side of a nuke.

Someone on Sterling Squadron (Ethan suspected Angel) had secretly painted shark teeth and red eyes on the devices. Dr. Irving had approved.

Each bomb would explode twice. First, it blew up on contact, thanks to the small, precisely shaped charge inside the tank. This vaporized the fuel and dispersed it over a huge area. A moment later, a second charge detonated to combust the fuel. The resulting explosive pressure wave from all the stuff burning at once would have enough force to flatten dozens of buildings.

It'd make the one Angel had dropped and lit with her laser seem like a firecracker in comparison.

Dr. Irving had taken Ethan aside the night before and cautioned him, "The lethal concussive radius of these bombs might exceed the top-exit velocity of the delivery I.C.E."

Ethan got the message loud and clear: this might be a suicide run for whoever dropped the bombs.

He was still working out how to make that risk as small as possible, but for now the best bet was Felix and his beetle, with the heaviest armor in the squadron.

"We better load the last of the robots onto the Luna moths, grab the bombs with our I.C.E.s, and move out," Ethan said. He took in a deep breath and added, "And I just wanted to say thanks to you guys. No matter what happens, humanity wouldn't have had a chance without you. Neither would I."

"No problem, little brother," Emma said, and punched him hard on the shoulder. "All in a day's work."

"We've always believed in you, too," Felix said.

"Yeah . . . ," Madison said. She looked at the floor, uncharacteristically shy. "Except maybe those first few days when you were screaming and hyperventilating every time you saw a bug."

Ethan grinned at her. He wanted to tell Madison especially how he felt. That after this was all over—what? He wasn't sure, but he had to tell her something before they left.

Boots echoed over the deck.

Ethan turned, recognizing the purposeful stride of Colonel Winter. Dr. Irving was with her, too. Neither adult looked happy.

Ethan and his crew saluted.

The colonel gave them a quick nod in return. "I'll just cut to it, Lieutenant," she said. There was something in her tone, *not* the usual steely chill, and it made Ethan worry.

"Yes, ma'am?"

It was one of the rare times that the colonel stopped and looked as if she was having a hard time speaking her mind.

"Please," Dr. Irving said, "let me."

"Very well, Doctor," Colonel Winter replied. "This is after all your area of expertise."

"Is something not working with the bombs?" Ethan asked, his worry turning into a stab of panic. "Have the Ch'zar found—"

Dr. Irving held up a slightly trembling hand. "Neither of those things, my boy. This concerns your preflight medical screenings. The results, which I tripled-checked, have come in. There is, I am afraid, an . . . irregularity."

Ethan glanced at his friends.

Emma looked as clueless as he was about Dr. Irving's words. But Felix and Madison looked as if they'd both just been punched in the gut.

"One pilot has elevated testosterone levels and other chemical markers that we know are precursors to . . ."

Then Ethan got it.

"Puberty," Ethan said, and his brain felt like it'd been hit with a hammer.

Dr. Irving and Colonel Winter were there to tell him he was going to hit puberty and he couldn't fly the most critical mission of his life.

There was no way anyone about to hit puberty could leave the underground base. Once out there, if the Ch'zar Collective got into their mind, the enemy would know the entire plan. They'd pull their forces in around the elevator and Sterling Squadron would never get a shot at it. Worse, the Ch'zar would learn the location of Titan Base.

Ethan took a step forward, shoulders back, sad, but proud. "I understand," he said. "And I'll do the right thing."

Dr. Irving held a data pad, numbers and graphs flashing over its screen.

Ethan went to grab it, but the doctor took another step—and handed it to Felix.

Felix read the test results, his face flushed, and he inhaled sharply.

"I thought this might be happening," he whispered to Ethan. "I . . . I'm so sorry."

Felix? Puberty? Ethan understood it, but he couldn't quite believe it.

And how could Ethan go into combat without his best friend? The anchor of the squadron?

Another part of his mind clicked on, and Ethan worried about the tactical considerations of his operation. He'd been counting on the massive rhinoceros beetle to carry three bombs. Emma's ladybug might be able to carry one or two more. Those two I.C.E.s were the only ones with that amount of lifting capacity.

"Are you absolutely sure?" Ethan asked Dr. Irving, almost pleading.

"As I told you," he replied with an apologetic shrug, "the lab results were triple-checked."

"It's okay, Ethan," Felix said, his voice suddenly as strong as it'd always been. "I had a great run as a Resistance pilot. Now I have to stay behind and help as best I can in the Command Center. We all grow up knowing it's got to happen eventually."

Felix and Emma then shared a long, meaningful look.

Ethan shook his head, still not accepting this.

"Emma can take my beetle," Felix told him. "The controls are a near match to her ladybug."

"I volunteer," Emma said, and held her chin high. She moved to Felix's side, wrapped an arm around him, and gave him a big squeeze.

Ethan felt numb and unable to decide what to do.

"Lieutenant," Colonel Winter said. "You need to issue new orders and shape your squad. We have a mission to run."

"Yes, ma'am." Ethan choked back his sadness. "Sergeant, I'm sorry, but you're benched. Emma will take

Big Blue and grab three bombs. My wasp and another I.C.E. will grab one more apiece. We should be able to hit a hundred and fifty miles an hour with that load, which still has us on time for predawn strike."

He looked at Felix, tears prickling his eyes, saluted, and then turned to Madison and Emma. "Get ready," he said. "We move out in five minutes."

Ethan then took Madison aside. "And about Paul," he whispered. "Tell him he's got his wings back."

Madison's eyes widened. "Are you sure? That guy is mental."

"Minus Felix, we're down one combat vet. I need Paul in his mantis with us on this one. Give Kristov the heads-up and tell him to talk to me if he has a problem."

"Okay," Madison said, shaking her head. "It's your call." She jogged off.

Ethan understood what Paul had tried to do the other day. He was just trying to get some "airtime" to figure things out. Ethan might've done the same thing (minus punching Kristov, though).

But was he going to regret trusting volatile Paul Hicks? With his life? And with the lives of the entire squadron.

○ ○ ○ 23 ○ ○ ○

OPERATION INFERNO

ETHAN KNEW THAT DANGER WAS ALL AROUND him, despite the oddly quiet jungle. There were no giant enemy ants crashing through the trees or buzzing locust I.C.E.s flying overhead. There were no birdcalls either. It was as if the native wildlife knew something big was coming here.

Here was a five-acre clearing in the jungle a few miles from the Yucatán Industrial Sector. It was fifteen minutes before sunrise, and the sky was gray and blue and streaked with cloud-lit orange.

Standing motionlessly, taking up most of the space

in the clearing, were nearly seventeen thousand maintenance robots. They were in a square formation one hundred twenty-five units to a side. There were a few other robots on the perimeter, antennae in hand, listening for the enemy.

The noisiest creatures there were the Resisters.

Kristov was by his locust, making last-minute adjustments to its wing hydraulics with a wrench, cursing at a stuck fitting. Grease smeared his big arms up to the elbows.

Lee was on the radio with Rebecca's bee squad, who were in the trees and in the air being the Resisters' eyes in the sky.

Oliver sat cross-legged on the grass, eating a Titan Base preheated meal of macaroni and cheese that he'd taken a liking to (despite the food probably being a decade or two old). He made the worst smacking noises as he devoured the pasta.

Angel and Madison were having a heated but, so far, nonviolent debate about overcharging the robots' energy weapons for extra damage.

Paul polished the eyes of his Crusher mantis. He looked perfectly as ease, like he was washing the family car, not like he was about to go into battle.

Rebecca gave orders to one robot, who was translating those last-minute updates to its subcaptains throughout the robotic ranks. She looked comfortable giving orders, and Ethan thought one day she could be the next colonel.

Emma had the rhinoceros beetle's cockpit open and ran through its operation manual one last time. She'd said she had it down pat, but she wasn't leaving any details to chance this time.

And oddly the one who *wasn't* here took up most of Ethan's thinking.

Felix . . . How was he going to pull this off without him? Benching him had been the right call. If Felix had turned into part of the Ch'zar Collective out there . . . Ethan shuddered. That would've been a disaster they wouldn't have recovered from.

Ethan motioned for everyone to gather around him.

"We're as ready as we'll ever be," Ethan told them, "to execute what Colonel Winter has named Operation Inferno. The sun's coming up in a few minutes, and we need to be in the air and flying due east into it. Rebecca, is your squadron ready?"

"Yes, sir," Rebecca said. "Half will be with you, two more high in the sky, and the rest scattered at midlevel altitudes, all camouflaged and reporting strategic up-dates."

"Good," Ethan said. "The rest of you know the plan, and the recent changes?"

They all nodded. The squadron (except Paul) looked nervous and twitchy.

Ethan didn't waver as he met their gazes. He didn't let them see any of the fear bubbling inside him. He couldn't. They needed him to be resolute and sure they could win this fight today.

It was the least he could do for them . . . considering they might not all be coming back.

"Mount up then," Ethan said. "Wait for Emma to get airborne and we'll form up around Big Blue. Good flying and good hunting, Sterling!"

His people gave each other high fives, a few hugs, and then they broke and ran to their I.C.E.s.

Emma stayed behind to punch Ethan in the shoulder, but he stepped out of the way, and for once, she missed.

"Ha, you're learning," she said. "I'll get you next time, Lieutenant." Then she jogged to the beetle and clambered into the open cockpit.

The entire squadron got into their I.C.E.s, warming up joints and wings, in their preflight checks.

Everyone but Madison, who stood by her dragonfly, its armor reflecting a green glow onto her features. She spared a long glance at Ethan.

He waved at her, not sure what else to do, and she waved back. Madison then sighed and climbed inside her waiting I.C.E.

Ethan stepped into his wasp and sealed the cockpit. He was glad *and* not so glad that he didn't have to deal with puberty and the rest of the stuff that went with it. Not yet anyway.

He cleared his head and ran though his preflight check, including priming the self-destruct in case he was captured.

The wasp told him that it was ready and eager to get out there and fight.

Ethan knew that this time, it was going to get its wish.

The rhinoceros beetle took off, hovered, and sent dust clouds billowing into the air. Emma gingerly plucked up one, two, and then three of the fuel bombs with the I.C.E.'s six legs. Big Blue had to increase its wing power just to stay five feet off the ground.

Paul's praying mantis snatched up a bomb and maneuvered next to the beetle.

Ethan fluttered the wasp's wings, took off, and grabbed the last fuel bomb. He cradled it close to the wasp's abdomen.

It was scary to think how much force was contained in this thing. And *super*scary to know, if he dropped it, there'd be a flash and then he and his squadron would be blasted to flattened cinders.

He, Emma, and Paul rose into the air.

Kristov's bloodred locust took up position on their starboard side. Oliver in his silver cockroach was on their port side. Madison flitted to a location in front of them, darting back and forth. Lee and his nimble housefly had rearguard. And over them flew Angel in her black wasp.

The squadron was limited to the beetle's top speed. Carrying all that weight, this wasn't going to be a supersonic-buzz bomb run. It had to be slow and sure.

They got to three hundred feet and headed east, building speed.

Now over the jungle's tree line, Ethan saw that the war still raged in the Industrial Sector. Ant lion artillery peppered the air near clouds of hornets. Fire burned everywhere. Scattered explosions flared like a Fourth of July fireworks show. A hundred smoke pillars rose black into the sky. They looked like pictures Ethan had seen of wavering underwater kelp forests.

The Ch'zar were still trying to kill each other for these last resources. Good. Maybe they'd ignore a few innocent-looking I.C.E.s in the air not bothering anyone.

"Rebecca, status?" Ethan asked over the radio.

"Camouflaged bees are in the air," she replied. "I've got four in randomly shifting positions near your formation. They're already bouncing radar pings from air and ground units. So far, successfully. Just don't count on that lasting forever, Lieutenant."

"Understood," Ethan replied. "Proceed with the next phase of Operation Inferno."

"Relaying orders to the boys now," Rebecca told him. "Give 'em heck, guys."

∘ ∘ ∘ 24 ∘ ∘ ∘

TIDE OF BATTLE

On his viewscreen, Ethan watched almost seventeen thousand robots roll out of the clearing, toppling over the trees that had been precut. They were a massive horde of wheels and sparking weapons and glistening camera lenses.

The robot army trampled every plant as they headed for the nearby six-lane highway used by the Ch'zar trucks. Once their rubber tires hit the asphalt, the robots really took off—accelerating to fifty miles an hour.

Ethan switched to his forward camera. It was twenty miles to their target—a landscape of factories, warehouses, oil refineries, and toxic-waste lakes, crisscrossed with a network of roads, railways, and conveyor belts. It didn't look like the Earth he knew. It looked more like a mechanized world.

"Level out at five hundred feet," he ordered over the radio.

That was high enough to clear the smokestacks and towers. It was low enough to zip over any ground-based enemy units. Ethan and his squad would flash over their heads too fast to make good targets.

Their formation hit five hundred feet and together they gradually accelerated forward.

Ethan checked on the robots.

On-screen he saw the first wave hit the outskirts of the Industrial Sector. There was a battle in progress between fifty red army ant I.C.E.s, each the size of a milk truck, versus six Shiva-class locusts.

It was an even match because that type of combat locust had heavy armor and grenade launchers that they could fire at point-blank range. The ants had sheer numbers working in their favor.

The two sides were locked in close combat when the robots found them.

At first, the Ch'zar I.C.E.s ignored them . . . that is,

until the robots fired sonic- and rail gun–rifles at them. The sound bursts cracked ant and heavy locust armor alike. The magnetically accelerated bullets from the rail guns *spang*ed off the I.C.E.s, but as the sonic weapons cracked their armor, the bullets got through and a half dozen ants and even one locust dropped.

Ethan hadn't been sure they'd be able to do it. He was glad he'd been wrong.

The ants and locusts then realized there was a third force to deal with. They turned to face the robots.

But it was too late.

There were now a hundred robots speeding to them from roads and platforms around the warehouses. They opened fire and rained destruction onto the I.C.E.s . . . and left only cracked armor bits and pulped insect guts.

Yuck.

It was weird, because the robots looked so tiny compared to the Ch'zar I.C.E.s. And Ethan knew he looked just as tiny compared to the robots.

"So far, so good," he said, and turned his attention back to Sterling Squadron.

The formation had built up speed to sixty miles an hour—wing power only, of course. They'd save the jets for a time when they might need them . . . if they were willing to trade stealth for power.

Below, nestled into asphalt and concrete mounds, were the telltale silver glints of dug-in ant lion artillery. Lots of them. Ethan saw dozens, if not hundreds, of the things.

But they were not reacting to the squadron's approach. Yet.

He instinctively wanted to pour on the speed. Or drop lower so the enemy would have even less reaction time to spot them, aim, and fire. But any lower and they'd have to dodge smokestacks and towers.

The wasp's agility carrying the full extra fuel tank wasn't good. Ethan doubted he could do anything fancy like a roll or high-g combat turn.

"Emma," he asked, "how's the maneuverability of the beetle?"

"Like driving a truck on rails," she said. "Underwater. If I had five miles I think I could probably make a thirty-degree turn."

"Roger that."

So they were on a straight-line approach. He hoped the Ch'zar never figured that out. It'd make aiming simple.

Ethan had an urge to rip off his gloves and bite his nails—something he hadn't done since he was a little kid.

He checked back on the robots and got three separate video feeds from Rebecca's bee units in the air over the region.

Thousands of robots poured through the Industrial Sector. From the first view at three thousand feet they looked like a glittering metallic tide sweeping in and crashing over grounded hornet I.C.E.s, locusts, and army ants. There were sparks and the flares of flamethrowers.

Nothing seemed to slow the mechanized blitzkrieg.

The second view was from five hundred feet. A cluster of flamethrower-carrying 'bots had cornered a cluster of a hundred army ants. The ants tried to burrow into the ground, but the robots closed ranks and fried the bugs in an ever-shrinking circle of fiery death.

The last view was from a rooftop. Ethan watched his robots going hand to hand with a locust. He thought that was pretty stupid because the I.C.E. just shrugged off their attacks as it snipped off their heads with its jaws. With so many robots on the creature, though, they did manage to slow it down, a bit . . . and then Ethan saw why they were attacking an I.C.E. like this.

A team of six robots came wheeling out of a warehouse towing a huge cylinder of liquid nitrogen. They opened the nozzle and sprayed the locust—freezing it solid.

One rail-gun blast and the I.C.E. shattered!

Ethan breathed a sigh of relief. That was sure to get the Ch'zar's attention and hopefully draw all eyes to the robots . . . and away from him and his team.

Sterling Squadron had accelerated to a full hundred miles an hour now and the landscape below zipped by.

It was strange, but Ethan no longer saw any ant lion artillery.

The Ch'zar might not want that much firepower too close to their main pipeline into space. Still . . . to have *no* defenses seemed overly confident, especially for the Ch'zar, who planned things out to the last detail.

Angel darted back and forth out of her overwatch position, coming close to Madison. Was she playing tag or chicken with Madison? Was she crazy?

Yes. But it wouldn't have been a bona fide Sterling Squadron mission unless it had at least *one* of his pilots doing something reckless and dumb.

"Station keeping, people," Ethan growled over the radio.

Angel must have heard the steel in his tone, because she immediately flitted back into her spot.

"The beetle's topping out," Emma reported. "Speed at one hundred twelve miles an hour. Unless I use jets, that's it."

"Roger," Ethan replied. "Everyone set throttle controls to one-one-two."

Their formation settled into a smooth wedge of uniform speed. If it weren't for the ground rushing past as Ethan looked to either side, it would have almost seemed like he was floating in one place.

A bit over a hundred miles an hour wasn't a *bad* speed. It just wasn't the Mach 3 he wished they were rocketing at the beanstalk elevator. Every second they delayed gave the enemy one more second to spot, and annihilate, them.

He checked on the robots.

From the high-altitude view he saw that the in-rushing robots had stopped. Ground explosions flashed along a straight line on the ground, and his 'bots weren't getting past it.

He switched to the view from a few hundred feet.

Hundreds of his robots advanced only to get blasted

into twisted limbs, spewing hydraulic lines and flat, flaming tires that wobbled and rolled away.

On the other side of the explosions sat I.C.E. locusts. They'd formed up and launched one grenade after the other. Behind them flashed the golden armor of Leviathan-class superheavy assault scarab beetles. The scarabs stood tall and shot over the locusts with particle-beam cannons, melting a dozen robots with each swath.

The souped-up maintenance robots weren't armored to withstand that kind of firepower.

Ethan felt a dread building inside him. The robots' one big advantage was overwhelming speed and surprise. They weren't going to last long in a stand-up fight.

This wasn't good.

The last camera on the rooftops in the Industrial Sector showed that even the ants were ganging up on them, too. All the enemy I.C.E.s were working together *against* the robots. The ants completed the defensive line by taking up a position in front of the locusts and scarab beetles. They held the robots back while the I.C.E.s with ranged weapons blasted them to smithereens.

Ethan had counted on the different sides in this

new Ch'zar civil war staying on their sides, fighting each other. Faced with this new robot threat, though, it seemed they were smart enough to set aside those differences.

"Lieutenant!" Rebecca cried over the radio. "My bees near you are getting at least a *hundred* radar pings. They can't deflect so much energy."

"That can't be right," Ethan protested. "There's nothing out here."

He scanned his forward viewscreen.

They had ten miles to go.

Below, it was all railroad tracks, multilane roads, whirring conveyor belt systems, and a thousand (relatively harmless) industrial robots stacking cargo containers.

The wasp's weapon-lock warning system blared, indicating multiple rocket-propelled grenade laser targeting sites on it exoskeleton.

And then he spotted what was pinging them, now targeting them . . .

A hundred locusts took wing ten miles ahead near the base of the beanstalk, a great cloud of death and destruction rising to meet the Resisters.

◦ ◦ ◦ 25 ◦ ◦ ◦

PUNCH A HOLE

ONLY SECONDS UNTIL CONTACT.

Ethan couldn't take his eyes off the hundred locusts in front of them, a buzz of purple wings blurring the atmosphere that spiraled toward the squadron.

His mind, though, hit its afterburners—sped forward to *think* a way out of this mess.

Shiva-class locusts were a heavy assault unit in the Ch'zar's arsenal. These black-and-purple beasts were lethal in close combat. Their jaws were their main weapons, designed to counter I.C.E. armor. It was an anti-I.C.E. unit if there ever was one.

In hand-to-hand combat, they were even a match for the Crusher mantis. They also carried two pods on their hind legs that launched grenades. They liked to use them at short ranges to stun and soften up their prey, and then close in for the kill.

Weaknesses? Did ugliness count? No, more than that, they weren't as agile in the air as Kristov's bloodred species. They had no long-range weapons. At these speeds their grenade launchers wouldn't be that effective.

Ethan might have actually gotten a lucky break, because it looked like Sterling spooked them. If they'd spotted the squadron and had a moment to think about it, the locusts might have waited and ambushed them as they passed over. Their leaps into the air followed by bouts of insect wrestling were a devastating tactic.

Of course, his "lucky break" was relative. The locusts still outnumbered Sterling ten to one. And every second the squadron spent defending itself was more time for Ch'zar reinforcements to show up.

"Ethan?" Emma whispered over a private channel. "What are your orders?"

"Stand by for orders," he said over the squadron channel.

The calm in his voice shocked him. It sounded like

another person than the real Ethan Blackwood, who was screaming inside.

He flicked to his aft-camera view.

He glimpsed farther back into the Industrial Sector . . . and that brought his turbocharged thinking to a screeching halt.

Every enemy I.C.E. among the factories and warehouses that could fly had taken to the air. They made a black wall of death that moved toward Ethan like a thundercloud. Locusts, scarabs, wasps, hornets, and mosquitoes—there had to be ten thousand bugs coming after Sterling Squadron.

There was no strategy that'd save him and his squad from *that*.

He snapped out of his panic.

Surviving wasn't the goal here. The strange thing was that Ethan was no longer afraid. He had one clear goal: punch a hole though the locusts ahead so he could get to the beanstalk elevator.

There was *no* going back.

"Okay, listen up," Ethan said over the radio. "There's only time to say this once. Go jet flight. Madison, Lee, land on Big Blue and attach. You're going to help Emma go faster and maneuver."

Lee's housefly and Madison's dragonfly immediately zipped over to the beetle. The dragonfly perched atop its shell on the starboard side. Lee landed and clamped on to the port side.

Jet engines popped out in every Sterling Squadron I.C.E. and blossomed with fire, the flames focusing to blue-white intensity.

The firm hand of acceleration pushed Ethan into the contoured rest in his cockpit.

"Paul, you stick with me. We're going to ride shotgun with Emma and take out any locusts that get close to her."

"Roger that," Paul said, and the mantis drifted closer.

Ethan felt like he'd made the right call to bring Paul. It wasn't the mantis's strength that made him feel that way either. He knew Paul was a fighter (sometimes fighting Ethan), but Paul wouldn't let him down now that they were betting everything on this mission.

Ethan had the wasp curl its stinger laser to point forward, wrapping around the bomb. He hoped the heat didn't set the thing off.

"The rest of you scatter and fight, but keep up. We have to get to the beanstalk at any cost."

Green status lights flashed on his computer screen from the squadron.

Ethan was so grateful for every single one of them. They'd followed his orders. They'd fought for him. They'd even gone to the brig for mutiny. And now, entering this battle . . . well, Ethan couldn't have asked for better pilots, or better friends.

Laser targeting rings danced over the wasp's forward screen. There were so many inbound targets it drove his automatic targeting system nuts.

He turned it off. What was the point? The air was so thick with enemies . . . he could fire anywhere and hit something.

He shot and blasted a locust full in the face with a ruby-red lance of light.

The enemy I.C.E. seized, tumbled sideways, and crashed into three of its wingmates. Not fatal damage, but the four units fell to the ground and were out of the fight.

The rhinoceros beetle's horns sparked, and its particle cannon blasted three locusts in a wide arc. Their heavy armor shrugged off the superheated plasma, but that's not where Emma had aimed the center of her beam. She got their wings, singed the rainbow membranes, and then they ignited. The three locusts impacted a water tank and disappeared.

Then Sterling and the central mass of the incoming locust wave met.

Ethan blasted everything that moved in front of him—the laser on continuous fire mode.

Multiple grenades detonated around the wasp.

Ethan slammed back and forth, and black dots swam in his vision.

The wasp flipped.

Ethan's pilot training kicked in. He unthinkingly grabbed the controls and got the wasp back to level flight before they tumbled out of control and hit the ground.

Alarms blared. Ethan saw that the wasp's abdomen armor had an inch-wide crack from stinger to chest, leaking green-gray goo.

Lee and Madison pushed the rhinoceros beetle in a right bank to avoid getting plastered by five inbound locusts on a suicide crash course. That put the beetle in the path of a radio tower—and the three I.C.E.s ignited afterburners to miss it.

They didn't. Big Blue was just too big, and the insect clipped the steel structure at three hundred miles an hour.

The tower shattered into steel splinters and sparks. The three conjoined I.C.E.s spun once, twice, and then Lee and Madison got them straightened.

Kristov, Angel, and Oliver rolled and banked, letting loose rocket-propelled grenade and laser fire. They did their jobs, grabbing the bulk of the locusts' attention. These were foes willing to play their deadly game.

Each Resister pilot had at least ten enemy units chasing after them.

They were great pilots, but even great pilots could only last so long with those odds.

It worked, though. No more locusts targeted the beetle.

Ethan blinked and jerked the wasp's controls, dodged a locust that had made a run straight at him. Its snapping jaws missed by inches.

He wished he could jettison his bomb and *really* fly.

But they were through. He, Madison, Lee, and Emma had made it past the locusts' first attack wave.

Ethan exhaled. His hands trembled.

He glanced at the aft-camera viewscreen. The locusts banked and headed back their way. Unencumbered by huge and heavy bombs, they'd catch up in no time.

"Ethan." Kristov's voice cut through a static-filled radio channel. "I have a locked hydraulic control. I can barely steer my bug!"

Ethan focused a camera on his position.

The bloodred insect was still in the air. Good.

But it was on a course up and away from the battle, thick smoke trailing from its port jet engine, and Kristov had four locusts on his tail. That was not good.

What was going to happen next played out in Ethan's head. Kristov would get hit and die. Angel and Oliver would stick it out, dogfighting until the same happened to them.

And the rest of the squad? There was no way to outrun or outmaneuver the locusts to get close to the beanstalk elevator.

They were *all* going to die trying.

Ethan had to drop these bombs *now* to even have a one in a million fighting chance to survive.

Drop the bombs?

Yes . . . that was exactly what he was going to do!

∘ ∘ ∘ 26 ∘ ∘ ∘

PATH OF FIRE AND BLOOD

ETHAN FLIPPED ON THE SQUADRON CHANNEL. "Listen, everyone. New plan. Angel, Oliver, catch up Kristov, get those locusts off him, then follow him on his present course."

"That's away from the battle," Oliver said. "Away from you guys!"

"Trust me," Ethan said. "It's going to work."

"I'm sorry, Lieutenant," Kristov whispered. He sounded ashamed, as if his I.C.E. locking up was his fault.

How could he know that even if he was in top

fighting shape for the battle, it wasn't going to matter anymore?

"Emma, Lee, Madison, you guys hit your afterburners, dump all the fuel you can, and build up as much speed as possible."

"It's not going to be much," Madison replied, "but okay."

Their engines flared to life, and they slowly pulled ahead of Ethan's wasp and Paul in the praying mantis.

"What are *we* doing?" Paul asked.

"Hanging back," Ethan said. "Gaining a bit of height . . . and then on my mark, we're dropping these bombs."

There was a long pause over the channel, and finally Paul said, "Yeah, I get it. The locusts chasing us get barbecued. That may be the first order you've given, Blackwood, that I actually agree with."

"We just have to make sure we outrun the blast zone," Ethan said.

"Ha, then I'll race you."

Ethan smiled. Somehow he just knew that Paul with his impossible bravado would make a game out of the most dangerous thing they'd ever tried.

The wasp and mantis arced up to five hundred feet.

Radar pings and missile-lock warnings sounded in the cockpit. Ethan immediatcly dove to four hundred feet. Paul followed.

The warning cut out.

Those alarms had to have been triggered by the hundred or so Vampire-class tick I.C.E. single-shot missile launchers clinging to the beanstalk. They were there to prevent an easy high-altitude attack.

This was as high as he dared to go. It would make for tricky timing.

Ethan knew that Emma, Lee, and Madison had to be far enough ahead to survive the blast. The locusts had to be close enough to get caught inside the blast. For Paul and him, though, it was going to be too close to call whether they'd get out uncharred.

He stared at his fore and aft viewscreens. The blue beetle was a blob of midnight against a gray morning sky. The pursuing locusts were a wall of swirling, swarming purple dots, getting closer every moment.

He glanced at his radar screen.

The locusts were closing fast. Emma wasn't flying a quarter of their speed.

He watched, waited, and held his breath, until the locusts were in range with their grenade launchers.

"Now!" Ethan cried. "Bombs away!"

The wasp and mantis dropped their bombs.

His I.C.E. popped up like the cork from a champagne bottle. Free of the extra weight, the wasp was its lighter, nimbler self again.

Ethan hit his afterburners and rocketed away, screaming for joy (or in terror, he wasn't sure).

A split second later, the mantis's engines roared with thunder.

Ethan urged his wasp to go faster while he watched the fuel-tank bombs fall behind them. Something that heavy took only two heartbeats to fall the four hundred feet—and then the tanks crashed upon crisscrossing railroad tracks.

For the briefest instant, he thought he saw the first explosion and the outer shell of the tanks shatter. The fuel inside puffed into twin clouds that enveloped acres of trucks and towers and yards of stacked cargo containers.

The secondary explosive ignited the fuel cloud with a magnesium-bright flash.

It was hard to see anything after that.

Ethan blinked and blinked until the spots in his vision vanished.

The aft viewscreen was filled with a wall of fire, rushing out in all directions at the speed of sound—engulfing and flattening steel containers, towers, industrial robots, everything, anything caught in its path.

There was no way he'd hit Mach 1 in time, no way his wasp was going to outrun the pressure wave.

That meant the crack in his I.C.E.'s abdomen armor would get torn open. And his wings . . . they'd get ripped off.

"Wings!" he shouted to Paul. "Tuck them in. Curl up. Protect yourself!"

This was a tricky thing for any pilot—even Paul. You had to angle jets just right *while* commanding your I.C.E. to perform a midair wing-folding-under-shell maneuver.

Ethan's wasp was annoyed at the order, but it obeyed.

Its wings crinkled like some weird organic origami, then tucked under its exoskeleton shell—and then it curled protectively about its wounded abdomen.

The firestorm slammed into them.

Ethan lost all control. Half his cameras went dead.

He blacked out—

And came back, bruised, blood streaming from his nose, ears ringing from what sounded like every alarm in the I.C.E. cockpit screaming at once.

His hands moved first, finding the flight control and trying to right the I.C.E. from a full tumbling spin. The wasp instinctively loosened its wings from under its shell to help stabilize. That did the trick . . . otherwise they would have crashed.

Ethan saw one furiously blinking red warning light. The external exoskeleton temperature. It was past the red line, but thankfully dropping fast.

They'd nearly been broiled alive.

He sighed and keyed the radio. "That was too close. Look's like I won the race this time, though, Paul."

There was no answer.

Ethan scanned the aft viewscreen.

Every tower, container, and robot for a half mile had been flattened, pulverized to paste. Past that lay a vast wasteland of melted, smoldering metal wreckage. There wasn't a single pursuing locust left in the air.

They'd done it! Now Emma had a clear run to the beanstalk elevator.

Icy dread then filled Ethan . . . because there was no praying mantis in the air either. No transponder ping appeared on his detector.

The mantis hadn't survived the blast.

Paul Hicks was gone.

° ° ° 27 ° ° °

ABANDON SHIP

ETHAN'S EMOTIONS TURNED BRITTLE AND SHARP and it felt like they cut him inside.

He'd felt like this before when he'd seen Emma taken from Santa Blanca by the Ch'zar, and when he'd watched the Seed Bank detonate and thought everyone had died.

Paul was dead. It was his fault.

No—he wouldn't go there. Not now. Not if it meant messing up Operation Inferno any more than it already was.

The wasp moved fast, quickly closing the distance

to the rhinoceros beetle, dragonfly, and housefly trio as they rocketed toward the beanstalk.

The orbital beanstalk elevator curved up gently, starting a mile from the center of its base. Calling it a mere elevator was a mistake. This thing was bigger than any human structure Ethan had ever seen or read about before. Even staring straight at it, it was almost impossible to sense the right scale, to grasp that it must have taken millions of tons of steel and carbon-fiber cables to build the base and tower. The main trunk soared into the sky until it faded and vanished from sight. It carried a dozen railcar-sized tubes simultaneously up and down—flashing along the skeletal interior with multicolored lights.

It was more *superhighway into space* than a simple *elevator.*

As Ethan approached the other Sterling pilots, Lee shouted over the radio, "That was the *biggest* explosion I've ever seen. Way to go, guys!"

"Where's Paul?" Emma asked.

Ethan didn't answer.

The silence over the radio that followed was all Ethan needed to hear to know they understood.

"We're ready to do our part, Ethan," Madison finally

whispered, her voice thick with grief. "Whatever it takes."

Ethan glanced at his aft camera once more, hoping he'd made some colossal mistake and that the Crusher green praying mantis would be zooming after them, somehow having survived.

But it wasn't there.

He did, though, see beyond the smoldering crater left by the fuel bombs, the other hundred thousand Ch'zar I.C.E.s still coming for them.

Ethan wanted to tell his wingmates something to inspire them in this terrible moment. All he managed was, "We've got to finish this. It's a clear run to the drop point."

Emma then spoke softly over the channel, "I have to do this—alone, Ethan. I know you're my brother, and technically in charge, but there's nothing you can do to change the laws of physics. If the mantis didn't outrun that explosion . . . neither will Big Blue. She's too heavy, too slow. But . . . I—I'll take her in."

Ethan let these facts sink in.

Emma was right (she always was right). Even boosted with the four of them, he couldn't see the beetle building the speed needed to outrun the blast wave.

On the other hand, maybe the beetle didn't have to outrun it. The beetle's armor might be heavy enough to withstand the outer edge of the pressure wave.

He switched his computer to view the squadron I.C.E.s' flight status. Kristov's, Angel's, and Oliver's I.C.E.s were out of range, but the outline and internal systems of his wasp, the dragonfly, the rhinoceros beetle, and the housefly flashed on-screen.

His heart sank.

The beetle's exoskeleton was cracked in three spots, worse even than his wasp. A few grenade strikes would have grounded the I.C.E.

That settled it. Emma *wasn't* going on this bombing run.

"No one else is dying today," Ethan announced. "Here's what we have to do. First, Emma, set Big Blue's autopilot to keep this course. Next, I want you to override the cockpit door and force it open. Madison, Lee, you get ready to catch her when she falls out."

"What?" Emma cried. "I'm not abandoning ship! I'll finish what I started."

"I'll guide the beetle to the target," Ethan told her. "You're right. The beetle won't survive the blast, but that doesn't mean *you* have to die along with her."

"Well, I'm not going to let you die for me," she protested.

"Listen, Em. I have a—"

"A plan?" she said. "I just bet you do. But I'm not an idiot. Even one of your plans won't change the facts."

"I don't have to," Ethan said. "I'll be guiding the beetle in with my command override. I'll have her on a long tether, so I'll be able to break and outrun the explosion. I've done it once before with an even shorter head start. I can do it. Just believe in me."

There was a long pause. The radio crackled with static.

The four Resister I.C.E.s jetted toward the beanstalk. The structure had grown so it filled half the forward viewscreen.

They were running out of time.

"And if I don't go along with your latest, greatest plan?" Emma asked sarcastically.

"I'll use my command authority," he said, "override the beetle's controls, spring the cockpit hatch, and eject you myself."

"You would," Emma muttered. "Fine. But if you get yourself killed . . . I'll murder you, Ethan Blackwood."

Ethan smiled. His sister would never change.

"Madison, Lee," he ordered, "take up position."

The dragonfly and housefly let go of the beetle's back, dropped fifty feet, and hovered to port and starboard under the beetle.

"And please, don't miss," Emma said.

"*No way* that's happening," Madison replied.

"Okay," Emma breathed. "Ready . . . set . . ."

The beetle's underbelly cracked and hissed. The wind caught the slightly ajar hatch and whipped it wide open.

There was a spray of cockpit acceleration gel and Emma fell—struggling, swimming, and tumbling through the air—and then Madison's dragonfly daintily snatched her.

The emerald I.C.E. arced up and away from Ethan and the beetle. Lee followed on her port wingtip as escort.

"I just wanted to tell you . . . ," Madison started, then stopped herself from saying more. "I mean," she went on, "good luck and come back in one piece, Ethan. Please."

"I will," he said.

But Ethan had a funny feeling that he'd just lied to her.

He checked his command override and linked to the beetle. There. He had it. It'd be easy to fly the I.C.E. remotely.

What he hadn't told Emma or the others was that his command override was meant only for basic flight functions, not the fine motor control needed to move her legs and cleanly release all three bombs at once.

For that he had to use his mind.

He'd commanded his wasp before at a distance. He was sure he could do the same with Felix's rhinoceros beetle.

He reached out with his thoughts and felt the beetle's slow, sluggish insect brain pulsing. While it recognized Ethan and his command authority, it also pushed back, expecting and wanting its own pilot, Felix.

Ethan had a special bond with his wasp that had grown stronger with every flight and fight. Felix must have developed a similarly strong attachment with his I.C.E.

The connection between Ethan and the beetle *was* there, but it was weak.

He would have to be right on top of it to guarantee he could release the bombs.

So Ethan was going to have to ride it all the way to the drop point . . . and this time outrun the combined supersonic pressure waves of *three* detonations.

... 28 ...

ETHAN AND THE BEANSTALK

THE ORBITAL ELEVATOR BEANSTALK LOOMED before Ethan and filled his entire forward view. The thing was a vast mechanical city unto itself crawling with robots and railways and conveyor belts and whirling gyroscopes the size of houses.

It must have taken the Ch'zar decades to put it together.

And he was going to take it all down.

Or try to.

Could he? Yes.

He thought so. Maybe.

Why then did Ethan suddenly feel like an impostor of the real Ethan Blackwood? Like he was a little kid playing at being the lieutenant of an elite squadron, fighting the bad guys? All make-believe?

He swallowed and forced himself to remember to breathe.

Ethan felt the fear creeping up his spine and taking over. Yeah, it was the fear of dying—he was practically used to that—but more, it was the fear of coming so far, sacrificing Paul . . . and failing.

He steeled himself. He wasn't about to chicken out now.

Ethan closed the gap between himself and the beetle, clamped onto its back, and ignited the wasp's afterburners. The two I.C.E.s accelerated.

There—just ahead. A red circle with crosshairs painted on his display. Twenty-two seconds by his navigation computer's calculation. It was the drop point Dr. Irving had selected.

The spot was where the gently curving base turned and angled near vertical.

Dr. Irving had assured Ethan that destroying this section would give them *the greatest probability for structural damage.*

Funny that Dr. Irving hadn't said it would *definitely* bring the beanstalk down.

Time for doubt, though, was far behind Ethan now.

Fifteen seconds to the drop.

Ethan pulled up on his controls, and the wasp and beetle sluggishly climbed. Every foot of altitude he could get would be another fraction of a second it took the bombs to drop . . . and that much more time for him to escape the blast.

Eight seconds.

At four hundred forty feet missile-lock warnings started. The tick I.C.E. single-shot missile launchers on the beanstalk had him in their sights.

Missile-launch alarms screamed.

Let them come.

Three seconds.

Two.

One.

Ethan touched the beetle's mind and ordered her to release the bombs.

The three modified fuel tanks tumbled away.

Ethan let go of the rhinoceros beetle.

Goodbye, old friend of my friend, he thought to Felix's I.C.E.

Ethan pulled up and rolled starboard—missing the side of the beanstalk by mere feet.

He twisted out of the roll, righted, and tucked the wasp's legs to make it a tiny bit sleeker. He had to squeeze out every ounce of speed so they wouldn't get roasted alive.

He snapped the aft-camera view to the cockpit's main screen.

The rhinoceros beetle plowed into the side of the beanstalk and cratered the steel construct. The missiles that had launched from the tower's defenses followed, impacted, and detonated, leaving a mushroom of fire and a blackened smoldering scar.

But compared to the rest of the massive structure, it was an insignificant pinprick.

Ethan then spotted the fuel bombs, spinning end over end, and plummeting toward the curved slope of the stalk.

They hit.

A flash.

Ethan glimpsed a half-circle halo of vaporized jet fuel hugging the beanstalk—

That ignited with a lightning-bright blast.

The air rippled outward from the explosion. The

shock wave was a rapidly expanding sphere—a white wall of supersonic, supercompressed air that could crush titanium like wet tissue paper.

Meanwhile, the steel and carbon fibers that made up the beanstalk sheered inward at the blast site, a gash that neatly severed the stalk a third of the way across. A hundred feet to either side of this the metal continued to shatter and rumple.

Up the beanstalk tower, Ethan saw the explosive impulse travel like it was a rope some giant had flicked. Steel struts and carbon-nanofiber cables snapped like rotten string.

All this took but a single heartbeat.

The gaping slash expanded and now severed half the stalk, and the white-hot metal edges continued to peel back.

Along the length of the beanstalk, following the initial pressure wave, a firestorm raged, sucked up through the central column. Steel heated and melted. Carbonfiber cables glowed like the filament in a lightbulb and disintegrated.

. . . And cracks appeared everywhere up and down the tower.

The entire beanstalk, to Ethan's delight, ever so slightly started to twist.

They just might have pulled this off . . .

Ethan's attention snapped from the beanstalk to the air—specifically the tidal wave of pressure about to swat him and his wasp.

He tucked in the I.C.E.'s wings and legs, curled into a ball, and gritted his teeth—

It felt like they'd run into a wall at Mach 2.

Blackout.

Ethan's senses returned, but jumbled.

There was a glimpse of his cockpit as every display and dial shattered. The wasp's exoskeleton armor crackled and snapped. Internal organs and hydraulics popped. He heard the insect's primitive war scream in his mind as it wrapped around the cockpit tighter to protect him.

Ethan came to lying beside the wasp.

The bent cockpit frame had completely burst out of the insect. Ichor pooled about the broken wasp. Its jaws and one wing still reflexively twitched.

Ethan rolled over, winced from what had to be

several busted ribs, and wobbling, got to his feet. He'd also broken his arm, but for the moment, it was thankfully numb.

He touched the wasp's head.

Only two tiny sparks of emotion burned within the primitive insect mind. First and foremost was a deep satisfaction at having caused so much carnage. And second, and almost an afterthought, it was happy to see that Ethan had survived.

The sparks faded, flickered out, and it was dead.

"Rest," Ethan whispered to it.

Maybe the wasp had finally gotten what it wanted: one huge mass of destruction and bloodshed.

He'd miss it. Ugly, terrifying, alien . . . and yet there had been some sort of weird bond between them.

He got dizzy, felt like slumping to the ground, but he took a deep breath and steadied himself.

Ethan looked around and saw he was halfway up a slight hill that rose above the jungle. Two ancient Mayan step pyramids stood nearby, half covered with vines. The air smelled of burning metal and a faint salty ocean tang.

The wasp had crash-landed and made a long impact scar that plowed through the jungle for a mile before it hit this hill and skidded to a halt. Most of the jungle was flattened by the pressure wave.

Ethan trudged uphill, each step more painful than the last, to get a better look at what they'd done.

Overhead he heard the buzz of insect wings. He squinted and spotted a giant fly and dragonfly. He waved at them with his one good hand.

The two I.C.E.s descended and landed on the hilltop.

He walked faster to meet them, no longer caring how much it hurt to move.

Emma climbed free of the dragonfly's embrace. Her hair, usually tightly braided and perfectly neat, was a total frizz-ball. Being whipped along at over a hundred miles an hour would do that to a person.

Madison and Lee opened their cockpits and dropped out. They all ran to meet Ethan.

There was a tremendous groan, though, and they all stopped and turned to see what it was.

It was the Del Sol Equatorial Orbital Elevator.

It hung in the air, moaning, metal shrieking and sparking. The ground-zero section of the stalk was completely severed.

Ethan could see *through* the gap in the beanstalk. There was nothing holding it up.

The entire length of the tower slowly twisted, shedding steel supports, cargo tubes, and threadlike carbon cables.

How was it defying gravity?

Ethan then figured it was because the beanstalk elevator ran all the way up into space, where gravity was weak. At the other end, for practical purposes, it *was* floating.

The part down there still had to weigh millions of tons. That had to drag it down.

It was as if the structure's buoyancy was a dream, and Ethan's realization that Earth had it locked in an embrace of gravity had woken it up . . . because at that moment, the beanstalk did indeed fall.

They watched speechless as miles and miles of the orbital elevator tilted in what seemed slow motion, then picked up speed. The base crumbled as the mass of the tower settled atop it. Huge clouds of dust and fire erupted.

The beanstalk fell over then, hit the ground in an accelerating line of obliteration, crushing railways, warehouses, and factories.

The higher parts of the tower picked up more speed, having farther to fall, and started an earthquake as it smashed into the ground as it continued toward the Gulf of Mexico.

It hit the great Ch'zar open-pit mining operation on the edge of the sea. It pulverized the massive dam there. Plumes of steam shot up a thousand feet.

The ocean then swept into the Industrial Sector and washed away every building and ground I.C.E.

The destruction was total.

The enemy wouldn't be building anything there for a long time, if ever.

Ethan gingerly took Madison's hand in his. It was soft, but hard underneath with the muscle and callouses of a veteran pilot.

She squeezed. He squeezed back and held on.

The airborne Ch'zar I.C.E.s scattered, confused and directionless.

Bits of the beanstalk continued to rain down. They must have been falling from the highest part of the structure because air friction heated them into fireballs that streaked across the sky in a spectacular display.

Fireworks for their victory . . . and to honor what it had cost.

"So," Emma asked, "I guess we won, huh?"

"For now," Ethan said. He looked at Madison.

Her sharp green eyes locked with his. "Nothing is going to be the same, is it?" she said.

"Everything has changed," Ethan replied.

OPERATION INFERNO:

AFTER-ACTION REPORT

Filed by Lieutenant Blackwood, Ethan G., commanding officer of Sterling Squadron

SUMMARY:

SUBJECT: CH'ZAR

The destruction of the Del Sol Equatorial Orbital Elevator resulted in a complete halt to production of the Yucatán Industrial Sector and to closing of the Ch'zar's main way to move materials into space.

It also caused major damage to the Ch'zar station in Earth orbit that was attached to the elevator. This dealt a devastating blow to the largest Ch'zar faction (designated hereafter as RED).

The other two Ch'zar factions (designated GREEN and BLUE) combined forces and used the confusion to strike against RED. Via the hijacked satellite network we watched a major space battle in which RED's almost completed mothership crash-landed on the moon with heavy damage.

Presently all three Ch'zar factions have resumed mutual hostilities.

Meanwhile, on Earth, major Ch'zar versus Ch'zar battles wage around manufacturing centers and the remaining three smaller orbital elevators. Enemy I.C.E. losses are in the hundreds of thousand of units.

Recon flights of Resistance scout I.C.E.s have been, so far, universally ignored by the enemy.

SUBJECT: sterling squadron

Repeated attempts to locate the Crusher praying mantis I.C.E. and its pilot, Private Paul Hicks, have proved futile. It is presumed that he went down or was immediately destroyed by the thermobaric device ignitions and resulting superpressured blast wave. The region is difficult to search due to the massive amount of beanstalk debris and flood tides that now cover the area.

Memorial service was held at dawn on the third day following Operation Inferno. Private Hicks was presented with honors. I left my resistor-bead cuff on his memorial plaque, which somehow felt like the right thing to do.

The remainder of the squadron has various injuries (see attached medical reports).

Spirits are subdued but positive and show signs of improvement.

Sergeant Felix Winter continues to adjust to his grounded status. It has been assumed that even though the Ch'zar are fighting each other, their influence over the adult human mind remains in effect. This has been confirmed by a minimal-contact recon mission to a nearby human town.

nOTE: Col. Winter and I are planning a follow-up mission.

SUBJECT: Insectoid Combat Exoskeleton (I.C.E.)

HIA. salvaged: Lt. Blackwood's wasp

HIA. missing: Pt. Hicks's praying mantis

ADDITIONAL: Two bee scouts, KIA. (See Rebecca's report for details.)

Dr. Irving has a breeding and genetic engineering program underway to provide new and replacement I.C.E.s ASAP.

PERSONAL NOTES: The loss of Paul hits me hard, but not like it would have before I joined the Resistance or started commanding Sterling Squadron. I honor his sacrifice and grieve that he's gone, even though we were never friends.

In many ways I am responsible. I was the one who reassigned him flight duty and gave the orders that resulted in his death. I accept all those things.

But Paul, more than any of us, knew the risks and wanted to fly and fight. He died for something. He died a hero, too.

Every pilot in the squadron knows they face a potential death on each mission. We accept that risk because we have to if we're ever going to be free one day from the Ch'zar.

Felix is adapting to life permanently underground, but it's hard for him. He's helping Dr. Irving with the I.C.E. development program. I expect with the doctor's scientific and military knowledge, and Felix's firsthand combat experience with the Ch'zar, those two are going to cook up some wickedly spectacular bugs.

Felix has also asked Emma out on three dates so far, and they seem to be a *thing*. On that note, at least, puberty seems to have some advantages (for which I'm happy to wait to find out).

And me? I continue to come up with new strategies.

When I told Madison that everything had changed, I was more right than I ever could have known. For the first time, we've gone on the offensive with the Ch'zar. The entire nature of what the Resisters are feels different. We're not just carrying out secret raids to hinder the enemy. We're not just hiding and surviving and hoping not to get found.

We're fighting back.

For the first time, the Resisters are at war.

And I, for one, plan to win it.

ABOUT THE AUTHOR

ERIC NYLUND is a *New York Times* bestselling and World Fantasy Award–nominated author. He has written science fiction and fantasy novels and comic books and has helped make many blockbuster video games.

Eric has bachelor's and master's degrees in chemistry. He graduated from the prestigious Clarion West Writers Workshop in 1994. He lives in the Pacific Northwest with his family. You can learn more about Eric at ericnylund.net.

Q & A WITH ERIC NYLUND

The following interview first appeared on the blog *Random Acts of Reading.* For the full entry, visit randomactsofreading.wordpress.com.

Q: The Resisters series begins with action and never lets go! Do you think your work in the gaming industry helps with your action sequences? Did your degree in chemical physics help in the imagining of the giant bug fighting machines? (Love those!)

A: I love those bugs, too. Thanks. I've always had an ear and eye for action, even in my first novels. Working for the video-game industry has honed that to a razor's edge—especially my work for the HALO series.

Having a few science degrees helped in imagining and designing the fighting insect machines.

What really influenced their creation, however, was when I was fifteen years old I was lucky enough to get an internship at NASA's Dryden Flight Research Center. For an entire summer I was exposed to exotic experimental jet aircraft, the superstealthy SR-71, and the then-new space shuttle, *Enterprise*.

Q: What made you want to write for kids, and how was the transition from writing books for adults?

A: A long time ago, I wrote a video-game prequel novel called *HALO: The Fall of Reach*. Soon after, I got a few emails from kids who said they never like to read, but they liked HALO and they picked up and fell in love with my HALO books.

A "few emails" became dozens, hundreds, and then thousands—and I found myself pleasantly surprised at being a gateway for a new audience into the world of reading.

After reading the HALO novels, these fans would write back, asking what else they should read. I'd suggest *Ender's Game* by Orson Scott Card and then the Robert Heinlein juvenile series, but found there was a shortage of good science fiction for kids. That's why I started writing for middle-grade readers. I wanted kids to have more good science fiction. I wanted to get them hooked on reading.

Writing for middle-grade readers is certainly different from writing for adults. It's economical: you have to tell a story with a minimum of heavy-handed techniques that you might use in adult fiction. Kids have an excellent ear for dragging, ponderous prose and they won't put up with it. My favorite fiction for the last few years has been middle grade because it's such an engaging experience.

Q: The Resisters put me in mind of the Tripods Trilogy and other classic kids' sci-fi. What were your favorite reads as a kid?

A: *A Wizard of Earthsea*, by Ursula K. Le Guin, *Ender's Game*, by Orson Scott Card, and most important to me, the "juveniles" by Robert Heinlein. These are dated, but so cool, and unfortunately getting harder to find. Some of my favorites are *Citizen of the Galaxy, Farmer in the Sky, Have Space Suit—Will Travel, Rocket Ship Galileo, The Rolling Stones, Space Cadet, Tunnel in the Sky*, and *Podkayne of Mars*.

READ ALL THE BOOKS IN
THE RESISTERS SERIES!

YEARLING
SCIENCE FICTION!

Looking for more great sci-fi books to read? Check these out!

- ❏ *Akiko on the Planet Smoo* by Mark Crilley

- ❏ *Boom!* by Mark Haddon

- ❏ *DarkIsle* by D. A. Nelson

- ❏ *The Ever Breath* by Julianna Baggott

- ❏ *The Last Dog on Earth* by Daniel Ehrenhaft

- ❏ *The Last Synapsid* by Timothy Mason

- ❏ *Mike Stellar: Nerves of Steel* by K. A. Holt

THE TIME SURFERS SERIES by Tony Abbott

- ❏ *Space Bingo*
- ❏ *Orbit Wipeout!*
- ❏ *Mondo Meltdown*
- ❏ *Into the Zonk Zone!*
- ❏ *Splash Crash!*
- ❏ *Zero Hour*
- ❏ *Shock Wave*
- ❏ *Doom Star*

Visit **www.randomhouse.com/kids** for additional reading suggestions in fantasy, adventure, mystery, humor, and nonfiction!